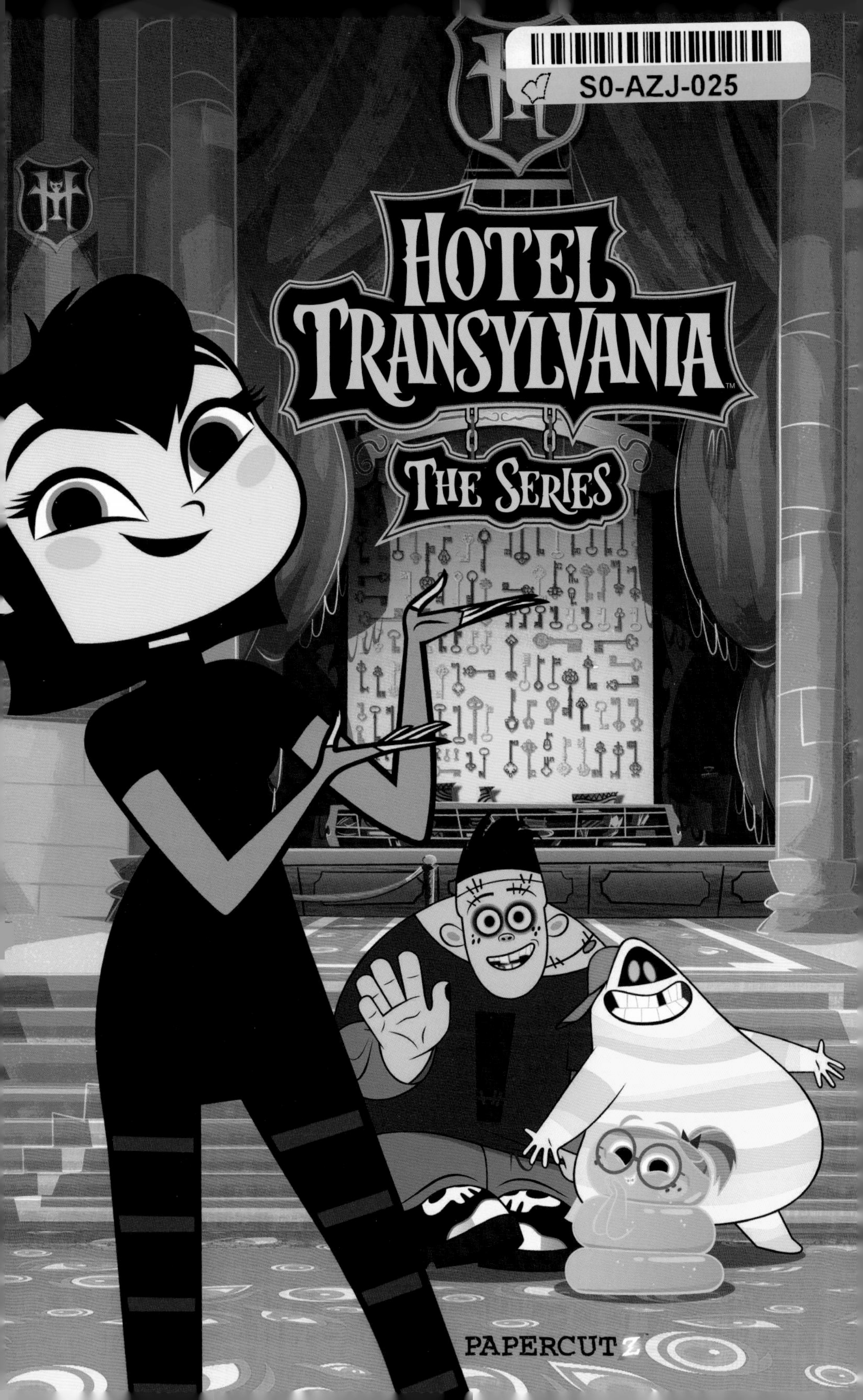
HOTEL TRANSYLVANIA™
THE SERIES
PAPERCUTZ

MORE GREAT GRAPHIC NOVEL SERIES AVAILABLE FROM PAPERCUTZ

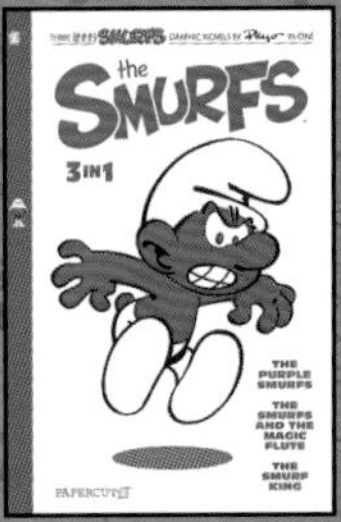
the SMURFS
3 IN 1
THE SMURFS 3 IN 1 #1

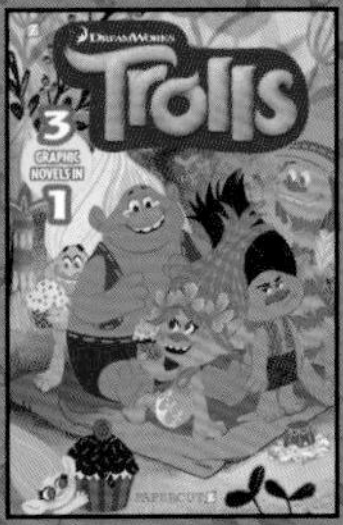
TROLLS
TROLLS 3 IN 1

COMING SOON

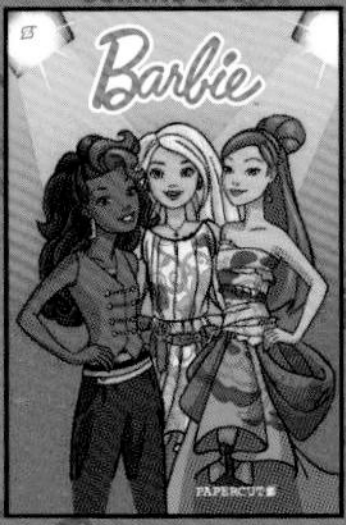
Barbie
BARBIE 3 IN 1 #1

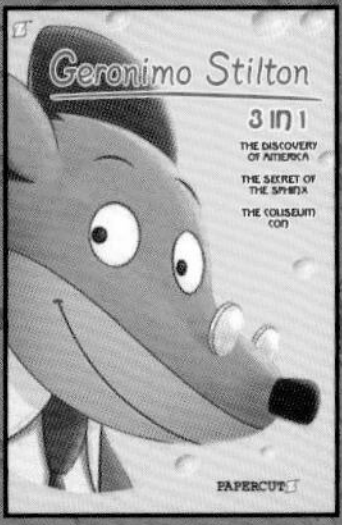
Geronimo Stilton
3 IN 1
GERONIMO STILTON 3 IN 1 #1

COMING SOON

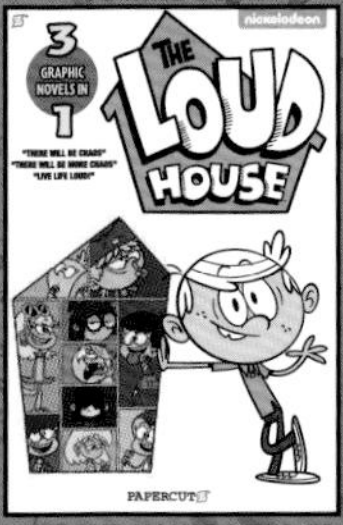
THE LOUD HOUSE
THE LOUD HOUSE 3 IN 1 #1

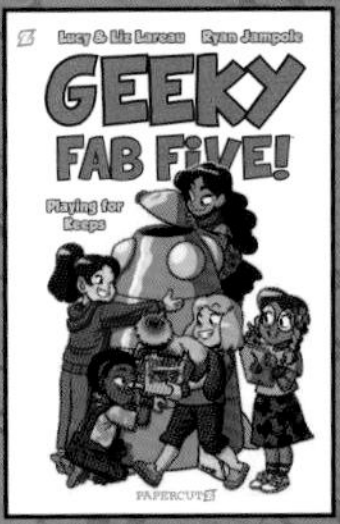
GEEKY FAB FIVE!
Playing for Keeps
GEEKY FAB 5 #1

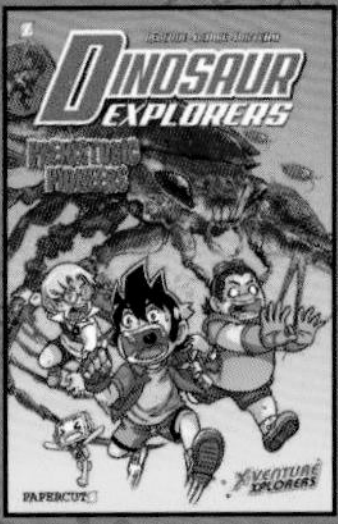
DINOSAUR EXPLORERS
DINOSAUR EXPLORERS #1

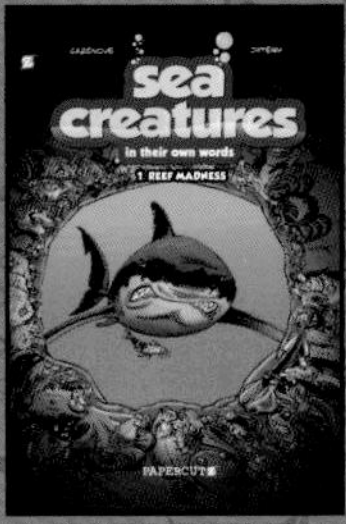
sea creatures
in their own words
SEA CREATURES #1

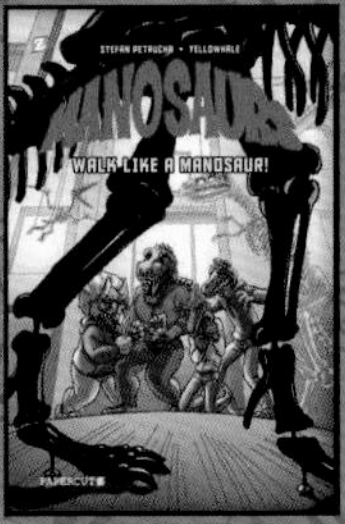
MANOSAURS
WALK LIKE A MANOSAUR!
MANOSAURS #1

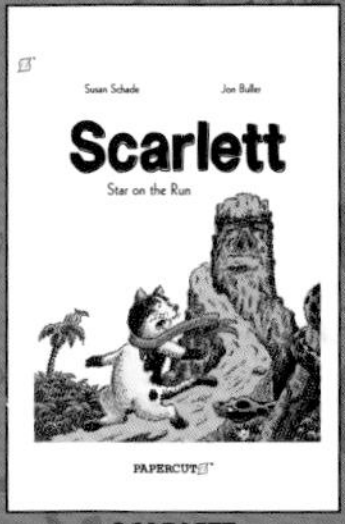
Scarlett
Star on the Run
SCARLETT

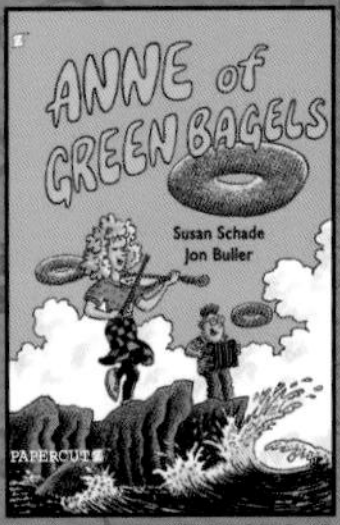
ANNE of GREEN BAGELS
Susan Schade
Jon Buller
ANNE OF GREEN BAGELS #1

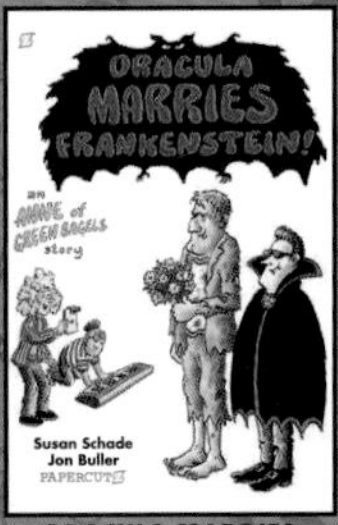
DRACULA MARRIES FRANKENSTEIN!
Susan Schade
Jon Buller
DRACULA MARRIES FRANKENSTEIN!

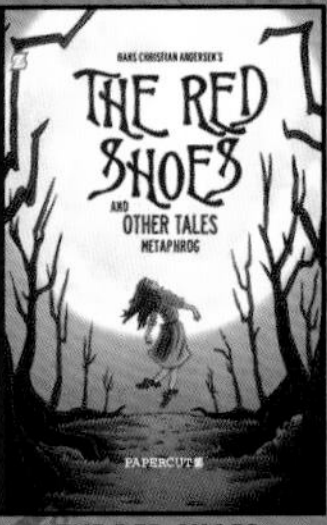
THE RED SHOES
AND OTHER TALES
METAPHROG
THE RED SHOES

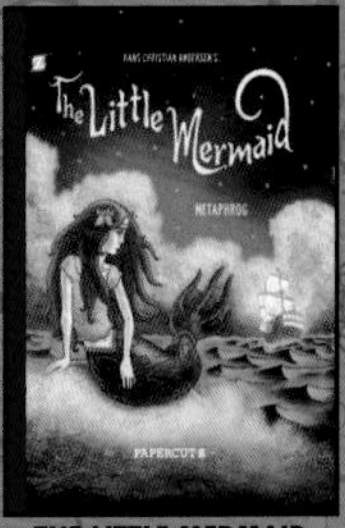
The Little Mermaid
METAPHROG
THE LITTLE MERMAID

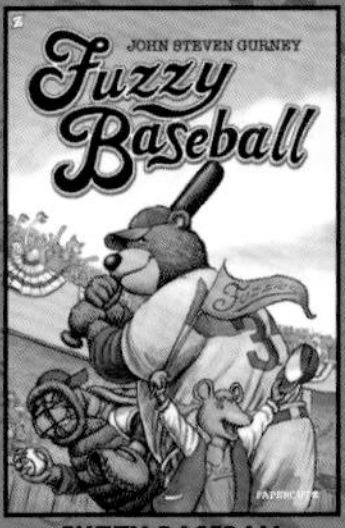
JOHN STEVEN GURNEY
Fuzzy Baseball
FUZZY BASEBALL

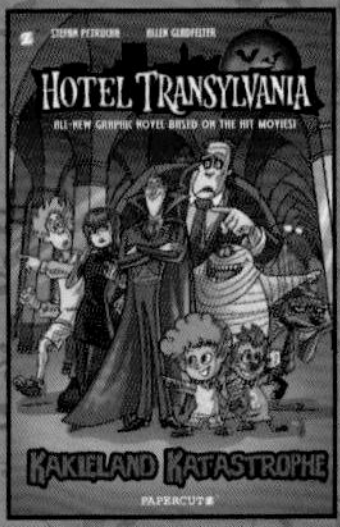
HOTEL TRANSYLVANIA
KAKIELAND KATASTROPHE
HOTEL TRANSYLVANIA #1

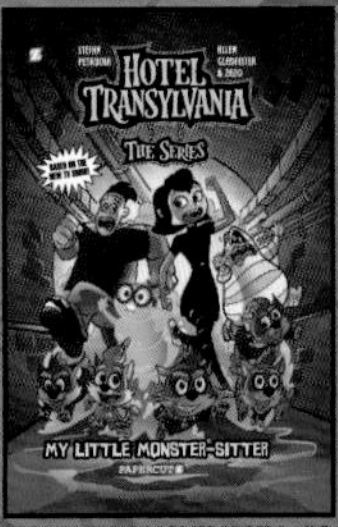
HOTEL TRANSYLVANIA
THE SERIES
MY LITTLE MONSTER-SITTER
HOTEL TRANSYLVANIA #2

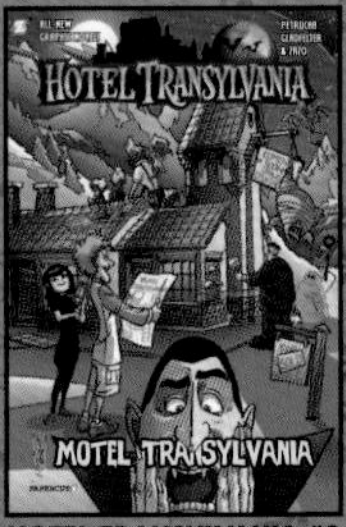
HOTEL TRANSYLVANIA
MOTEL TRANSYLVANIA
HOTEL TRANSYLVANIA #3

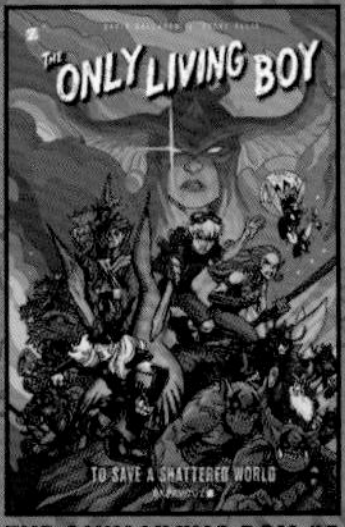
THE ONLY LIVING BOY
TO SAVE A SHATTERED WORLD
THE ONLY LIVING BOY #5

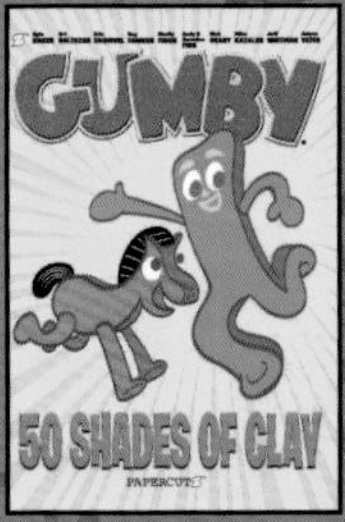
GUMBY
50 SHADES OF CLAY
GUMBY #1

THE SMURFS 3 in 1, TROLLS 3 in 1, BARBIE 3 in 1, GERONIMO STILTON 3 in 1, THE LOUD HOUSE 3 in 1, SCARLETT and ANNE OF GREEN BAGELS graphic nov are available for $14.99 each in paperback only. THE ONLY LIVING BOY and GUMBY graphic novels are available for $8.99 each in paperback, and $13.99 eac hardcover. DINOSAUR EXPLORERS graphic novels are available for $12.99 each in paperback and $16.99 each in hardcover. SEA CREATURES graphic novels are available for $10.99 each in hardcover only. FUZZY BASEBALL graphic novels are available for $9.99 each in paperback only. DRACULA MARRIES FRANKENSTEIN graphic novels are available for $12.99 each in paperback only. HOTEL TRANSYLVANIA #1 and MANOSAURS graphic novels are available for $7.99 each in paperback and $12.99 each in hardcover. HOTEL TRANSYLVANIA #2, HOTEL TRANSYLVANIA #3, GEEKY FAB 5, THE RED SHOES and THE LITTLE MERMAID graphic novels are available for $12.99 each in hardcover only.

Available from booksellers everywhere. You can also order online from www.papercutz.com. Or call 1-800-886-1223, Monday through Friday, 9-5 EST. MC, Visa an AmEx accepted. To order by mail, please add $5.00 for postage and handling for first book ordered, $1.00 for each additional book and make check payable to NBM Publishing. Send to Papercutz, 160 Broadway, Suite 700, East Wing, New York, NY 10038.

THE SMURFS, TROLLS, BARBIE, GERONIMO STILTON, THE LOUD HOUSE, GEEKY FAB 5, DINOSAUR EXPLORERS, SEA CREATURES, MANOSAURS, SCARLETT, ANNE OF GREEN BAGELS, DRACULA MARRIES FRANKENSTEIN!, THE RED SHOES, THE LITTLE MERMAID, FUZZY BASEBALL, HOTEL TRANSYLVANIA, THE ONLY LIVING BOY, and GUMBY graphic novels are also available wherever e-books are sold.

HOTEL TRANSYLVANIA™

THE SERIES

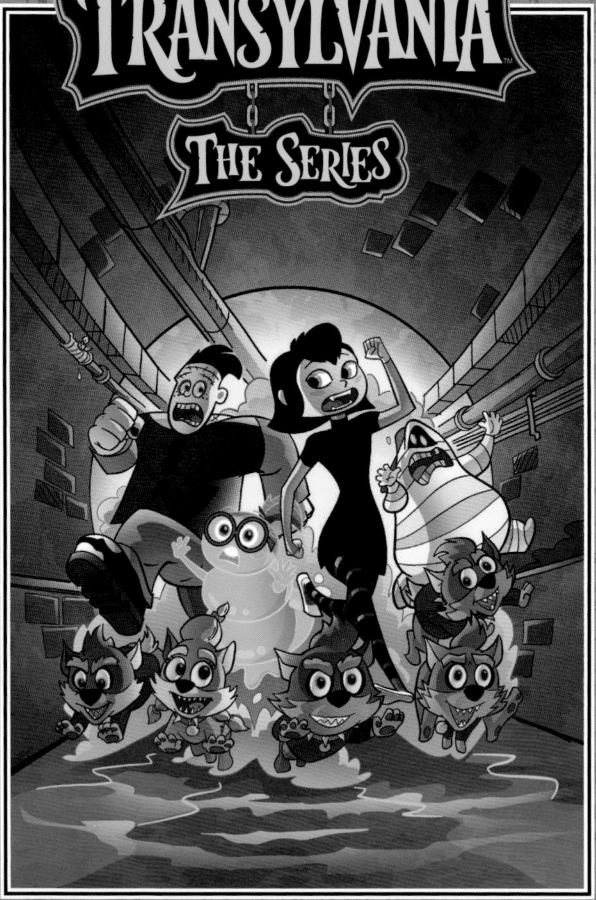

MY LITTLE MONSTER-SITTER

STEFAN PETRUCHA–WRITER
ALLEN GLADFELTER
& ZAZO–ARTISTS

PAPERCUTZ
NEW YORK

HOTEL TRANSYLVANIA
The Series

#2 "My Little Monster-Sitter"
Stefan Petrucha—Writer
Allen Gladfelter—Penciler
Zazo—Inker
Laurie E. Smith—Colorist
Wilson Ramos Jr.—Letterer
Dawn Guzzo—Production
Spenser Nellis—Editorial Intern
Jeff Whitman—Assistant Managing Editor
Jim Salicrup
Editor-in-Chief

Special thanks to James Silvani, Keith Baxter, PH Marcondes, Rick Mischel, Melissa Sturm, Virginia King, and everyone at Sony Pictures Animation.

Hardcover ISBN: 978-1-62991-855-6
Paperback ISBN: 978-1-6299-1854-9

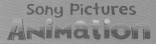
Sony Pictures
Animation

Papercutz books may be purchased for business or promotional use.
For information on bulk purchases please contact Macmillan Corporate
and Premium Sales Department at (800) 221-795 x5442.

Printed in China
June 2019

Distributed by Macmillan
First Printing

MAVIS

She's the natural born leader of her friends. Mavis is 114 ¾ years old and is in full-on teenage mode: She's moody, a know-it-all, and fearless to a fault.

She's also inventive, driven, and desperate to prove she's ready for more adult responsibilities.

HANK

Hank is the son of the scariest monster alive, the one and only Frankenstein.

He's desperate to make his mark, all in order to impress his father and get an "atta boy" out of him.

PEDRO

Pedro acts like a kid on a permanent sugar rush.

His only purpose in life is to have fun.

Which is kind of a goal, so fine – he has one goal.

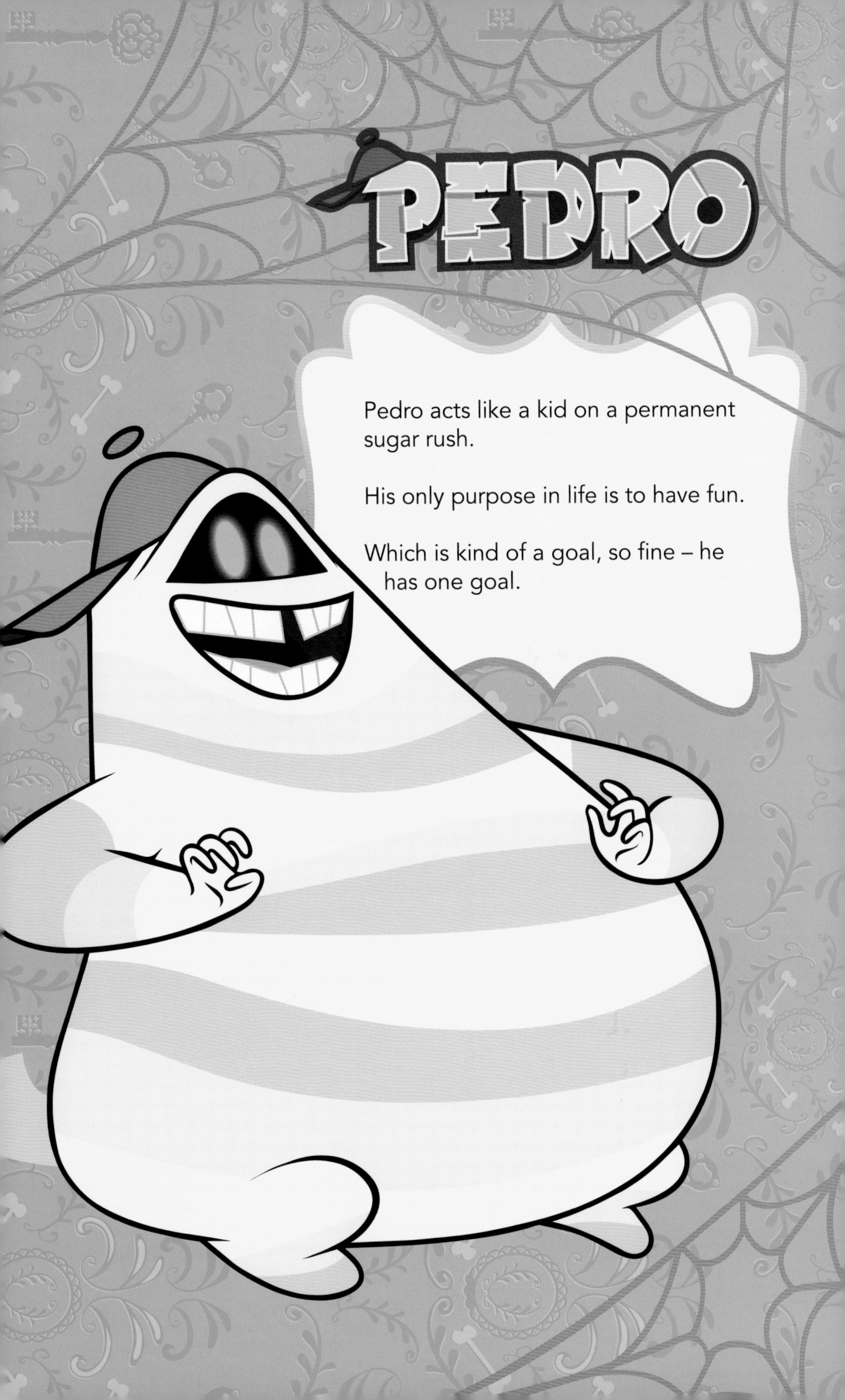

WENDY

She is Mavis's closest contemporary and confidante. In contrast to Mavis, Wendy is shy and awkward.

She speaks with a bit of a lisp and sometimes her "s" words come with a bit of blobby spittle.

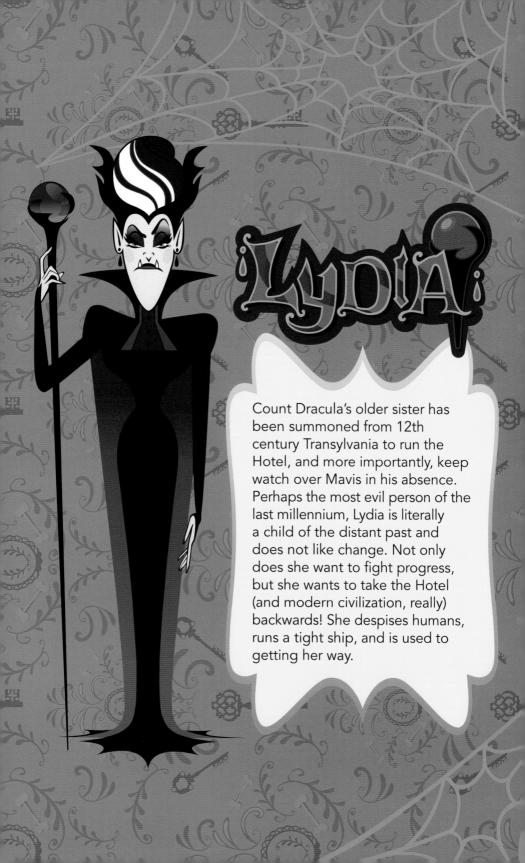

LYDIA

Count Dracula's older sister has been summoned from 12th century Transylvania to run the Hotel, and more importantly, keep watch over Mavis in his absence. Perhaps the most evil person of the last millennium, Lydia is literally a child of the distant past and does not like change. Not only does she want to fight progress, but she wants to take the Hotel (and modern civilization, really) backwards! She despises humans, runs a tight ship, and is used to getting her way.

WOLF PUPS

These rambunctious little pups have the run of the Hotel. Since they never stay in one place very long though, even their parents, Wayne and Wanda have lost track of how many there are!

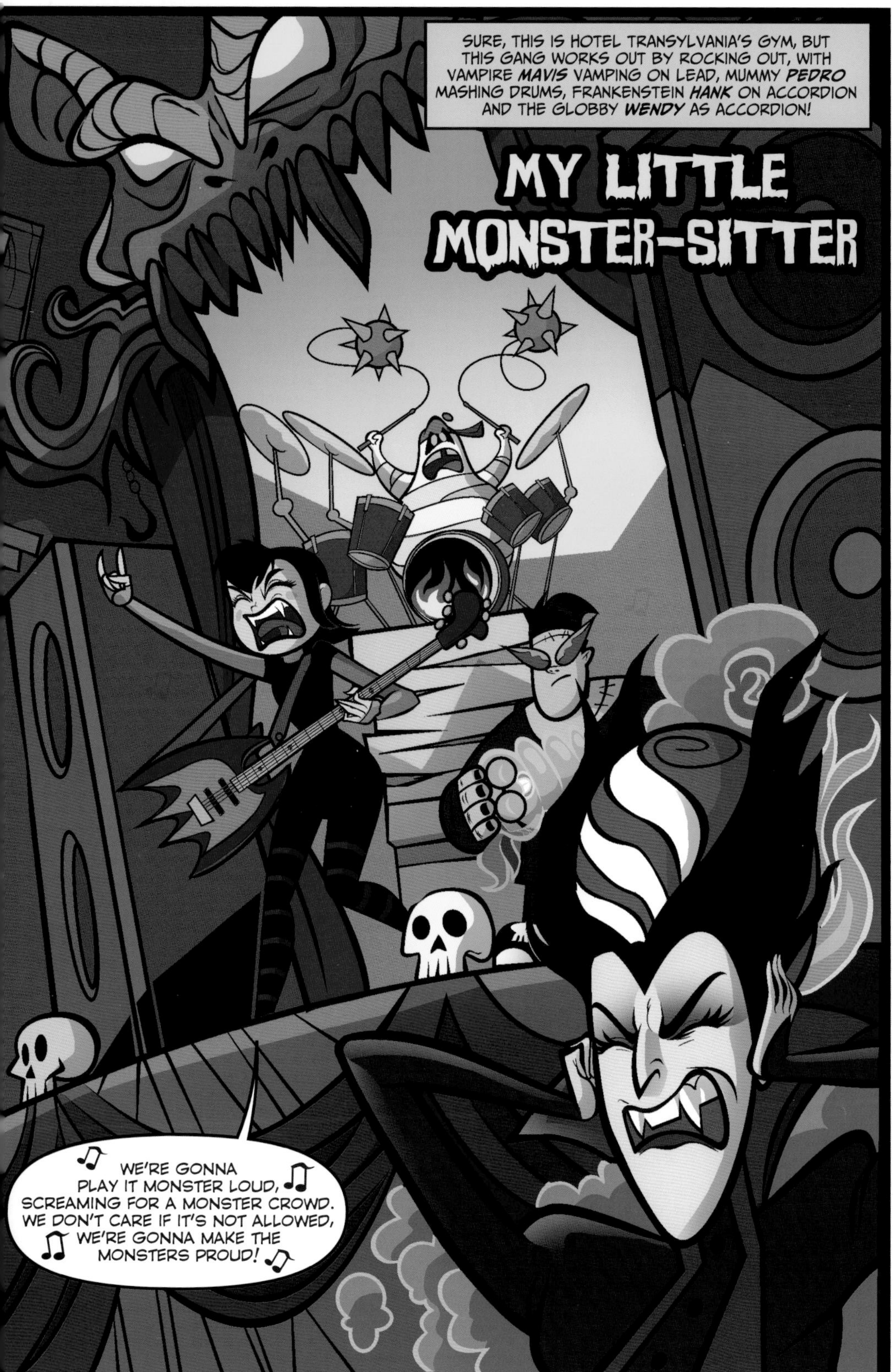
SURE, THIS IS HOTEL TRANSYLVANIA'S GYM, BUT THIS GANG WORKS OUT BY ROCKING OUT, WITH VAMPIRE *MAVIS* VAMPING ON LEAD, MUMMY *PEDRO* MASHING DRUMS, FRANKENSTEIN *HANK* ON ACCORDION AND THE GLOBBY *WENDY* AS ACCORDION!
MY LITTLE MONSTER-SITTER
♫ WE'RE GONNA PLAY IT MONSTER LOUD, ♫ SCREAMING FOR A MONSTER CROWD. WE DON'T CARE IF IT'S NOT ALLOWED, ♫ WE'RE GONNA MAKE THE MONSTERS PROUD! ♫

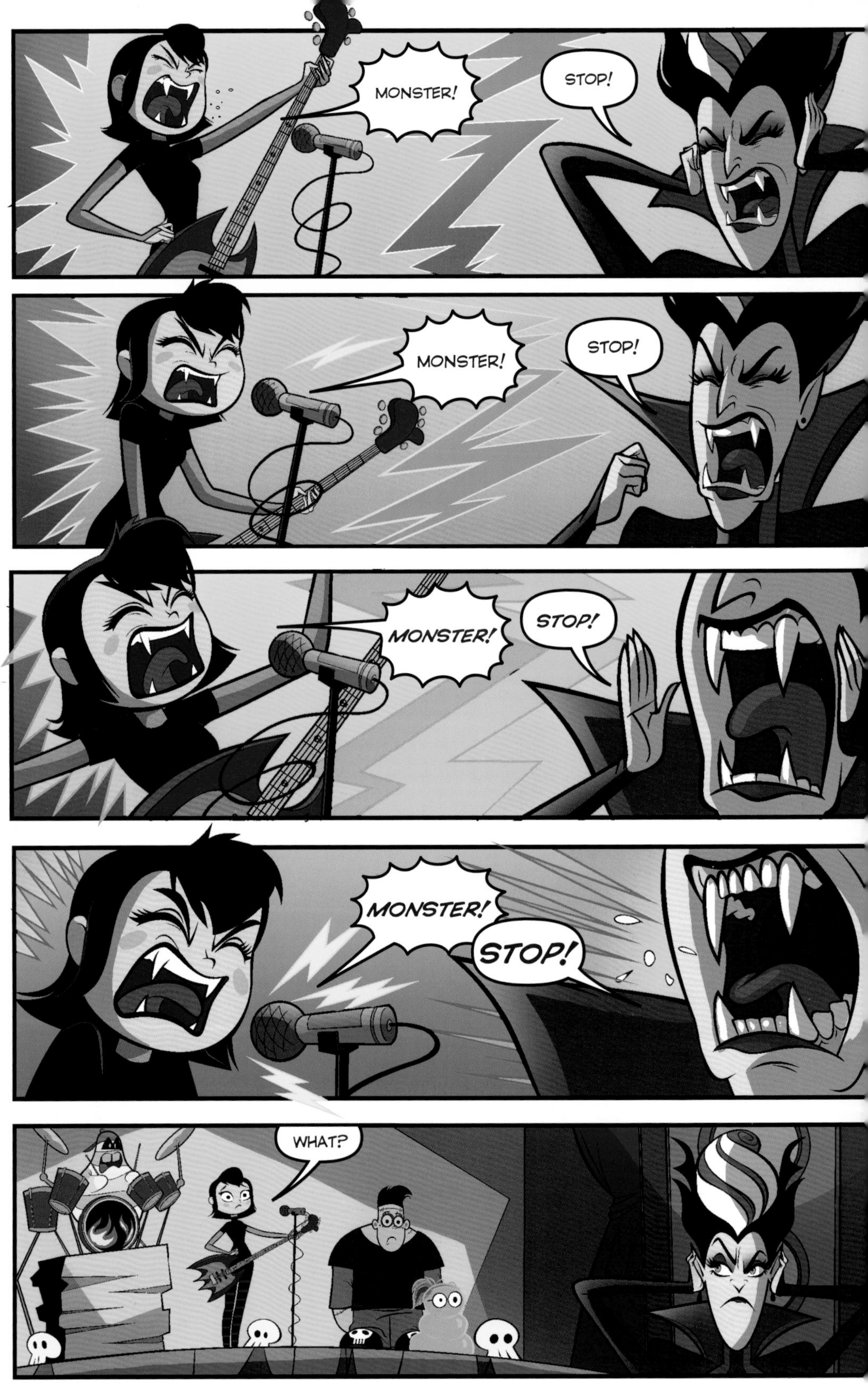
MONSTER!
STOP!
MONSTER!
STOP!
MONSTER!
STOP!
MONSTER!
STOP!
WHAT?

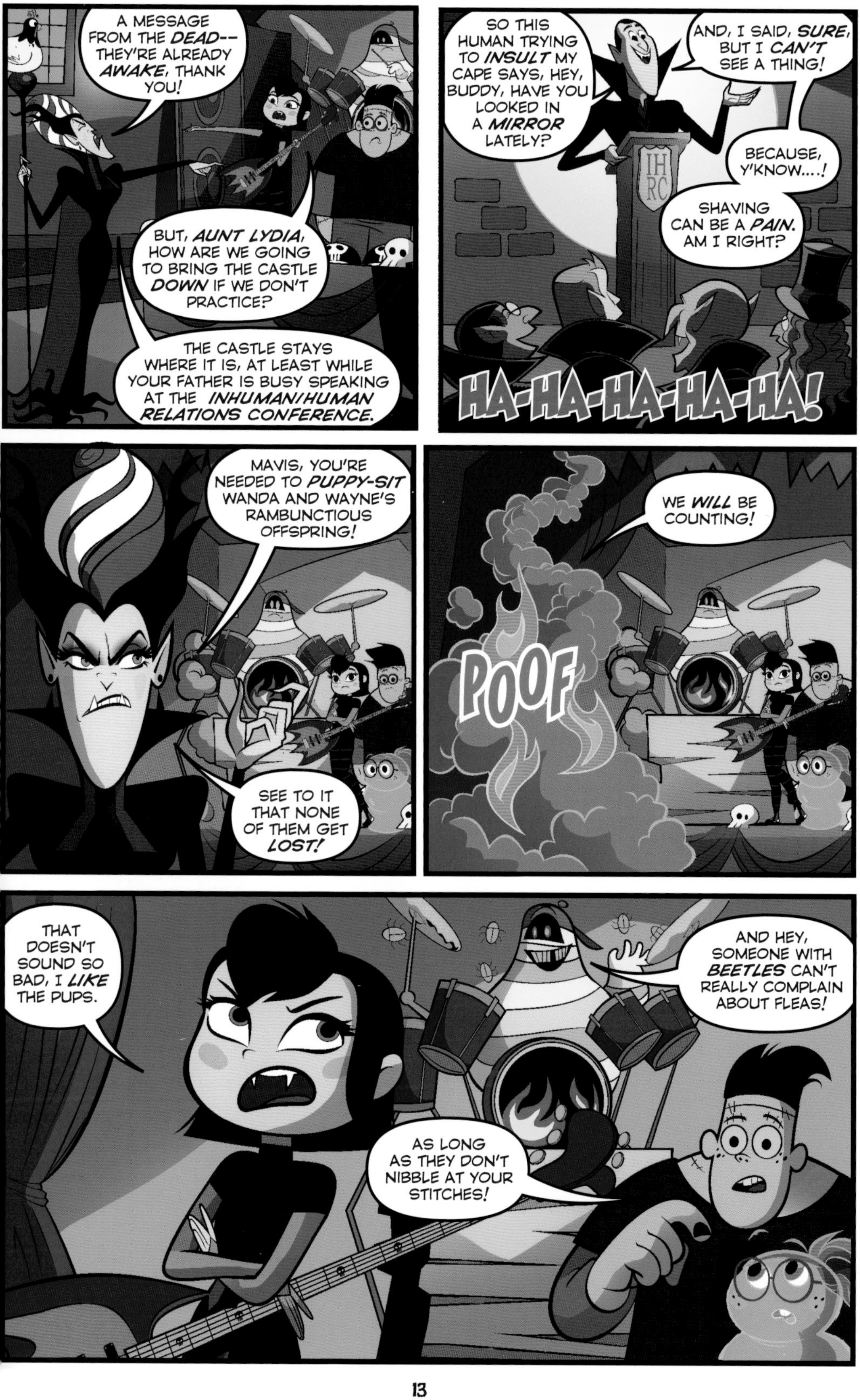
A MESSAGE FROM THE DEAD-- THEY'RE ALREADY AWAKE, THANK YOU!
BUT, AUNT LYDIA, HOW ARE WE GOING TO BRING THE CASTLE DOWN IF WE DON'T PRACTICE?
THE CASTLE STAYS WHERE IT IS, AT LEAST WHILE YOUR FATHER IS BUSY SPEAKING AT THE INHUMAN/HUMAN RELATIONS CONFERENCE.
SO THIS HUMAN TRYING TO INSULT MY CAPE SAYS, HEY, BUDDY, HAVE YOU LOOKED IN A MIRROR LATELY?
AND, I SAID, SURE, BUT I CAN'T SEE A THING!
BECAUSE, Y'KNOW....!
SHAVING CAN BE A PAIN. AM I RIGHT?
IHRC
HA-HA-HA-HA-HA!
MAVIS, YOU'RE NEEDED TO PUPPY-SIT WANDA AND WAYNE'S RAMBUNCTIOUS OFFSPRING!
SEE TO IT THAT NONE OF THEM GET LOST!
WE WILL BE COUNTING!
POOF
THAT DOESN'T SOUND SO BAD, I LIKE THE PUPS.
AND HEY, SOMEONE WITH BEETLES CAN'T REALLY COMPLAIN ABOUT FLEAS!
AS LONG AS THEY DON'T NIBBLE AT YOUR STITCHES!

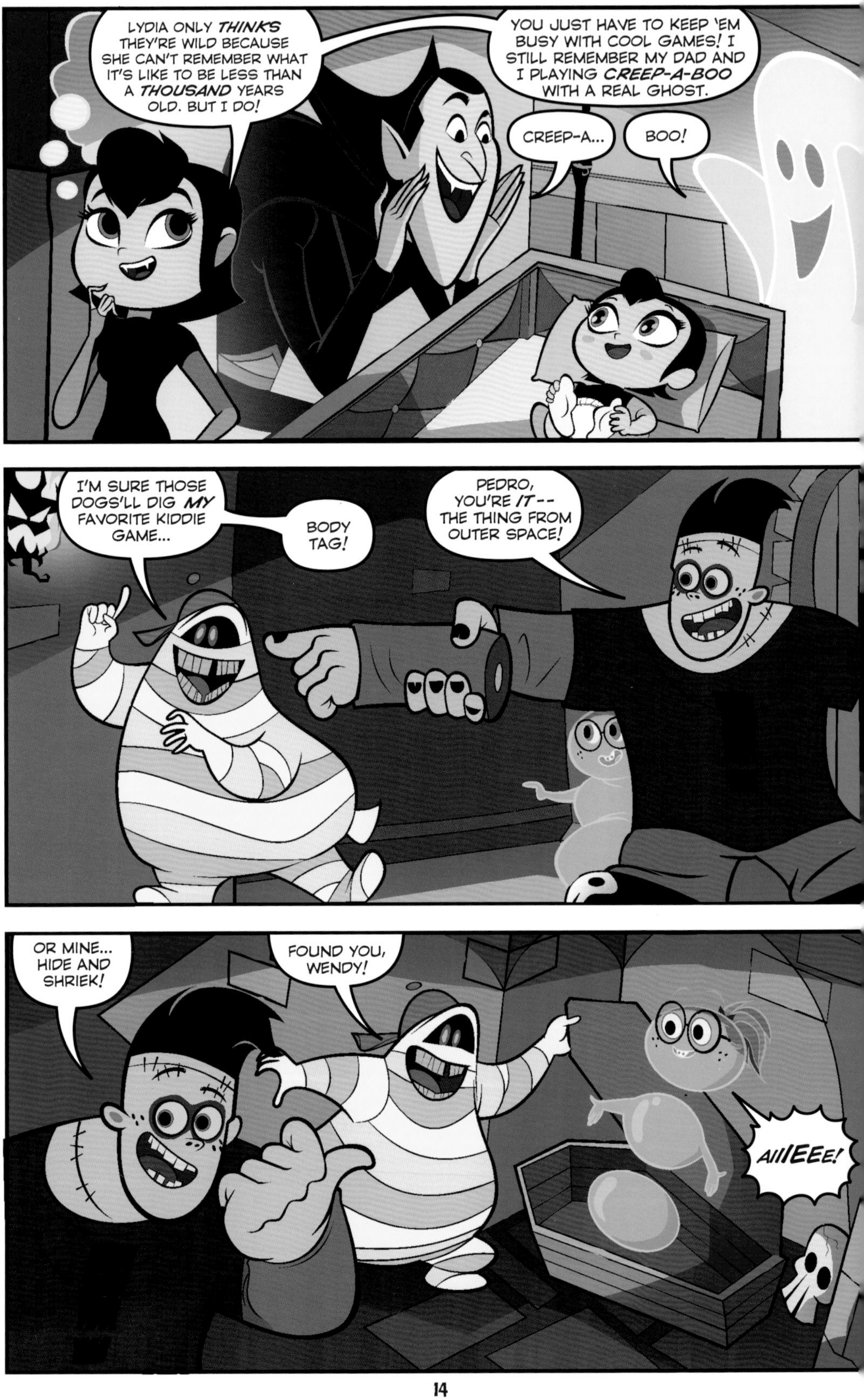
LYDIA ONLY THINKS THEY'RE WILD BECAUSE SHE CAN'T REMEMBER WHAT IT'S LIKE TO BE LESS THAN A THOUSAND YEARS OLD. BUT I DO!
YOU JUST HAVE TO KEEP 'EM BUSY WITH COOL GAMES! I STILL REMEMBER MY DAD AND I PLAYING CREEP-A-BOO WITH A REAL GHOST.
CREEP-A...
BOO!
I'M SURE THOSE DOGS'LL DIG MY FAVORITE KIDDIE GAME...
BODY TAG!
PEDRO, YOU'RE IT-- THE THING FROM OUTER SPACE!
OR MINE... HIDE AND SHRIEK!
FOUND YOU, WENDY!
AIIIEEE!

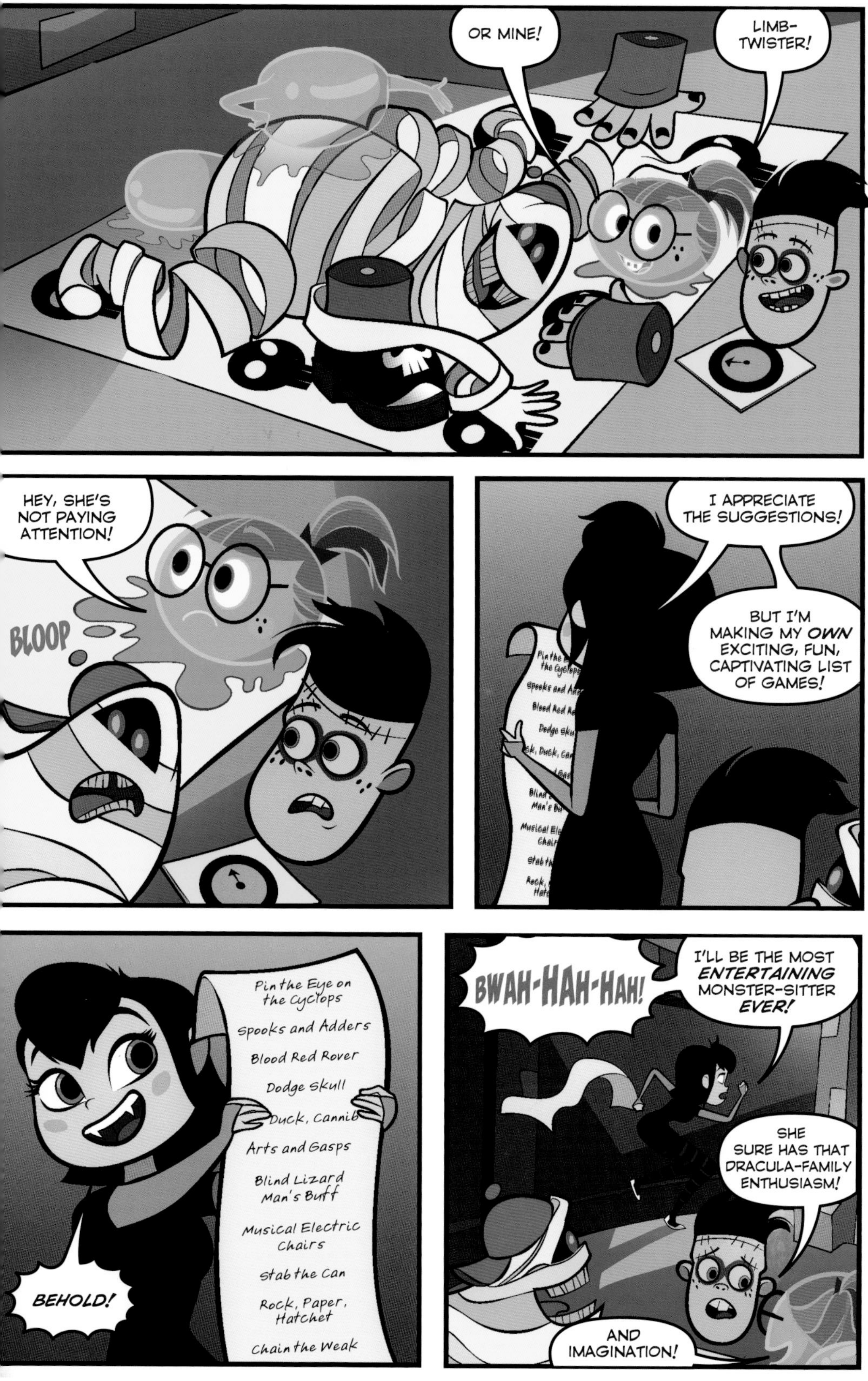
OR MINE!
LIMB-TWISTER!
HEY, SHE'S NOT PAYING ATTENTION!
BLOOP
I APPRECIATE THE SUGGESTIONS!
BUT I'M MAKING MY *OWN* EXCITING, FUN, CAPTIVATING LIST OF GAMES!
Pin the Eye on the Cyclops
Spooks and Adders
Blood Red Rover
Dodge Skull
Duck, Cannib
Arts and Gasps
Blind Lizard Man's Buff
Musical Electric Chairs
Stab the Can
Rock, Paper, Hatchet
Chain the Weak
BEHOLD!
BWAH-HAH-HAH!
I'LL BE THE MOST *ENTERTAINING* MONSTER-SITTER *EVER!*
SHE SURE HAS THAT DRACULA-FAMILY ENTHUSIASM!
AND IMAGINATION!

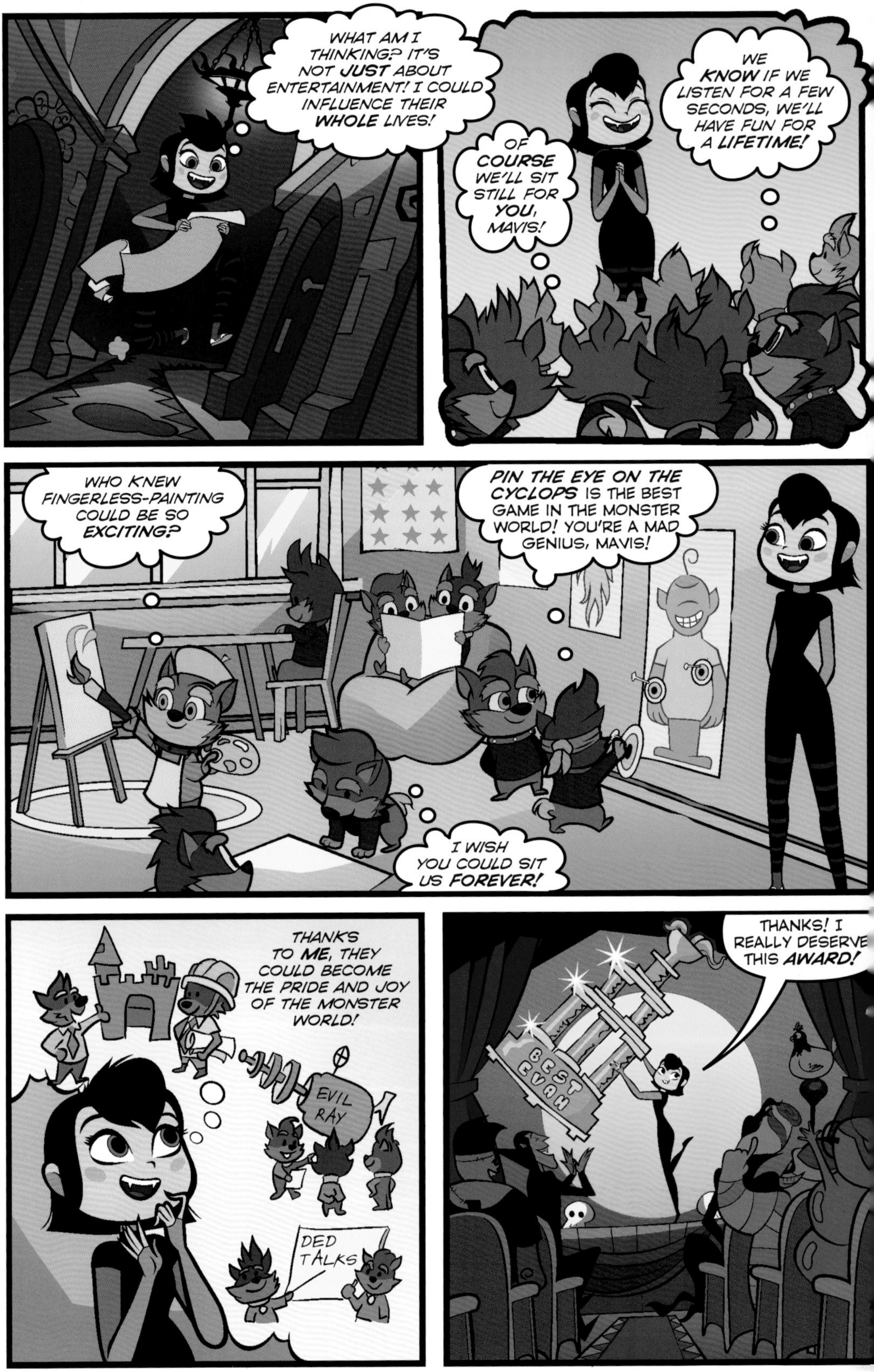
WHAT AM I THINKING? IT'S NOT JUST ABOUT ENTERTAINMENT! I COULD INFLUENCE THEIR WHOLE LIVES!
OF COURSE WE'LL SIT STILL FOR YOU, MAVIS!
WE KNOW IF WE LISTEN FOR A FEW SECONDS, WE'LL HAVE FUN FOR A LIFETIME!
WHO KNEW FINGERLESS-PAINTING COULD BE SO EXCITING?
PIN THE EYE ON THE CYCLOPS IS THE BEST GAME IN THE MONSTER WORLD! YOU'RE A MAD GENIUS, MAVIS!
I WISH YOU COULD SIT US FOREVER!
THANKS TO ME, THEY COULD BECOME THE PRIDE AND JOY OF THE MONSTER WORLD!
EVIL RAY
DED TALKS
THANKS! I REALLY DESERVE THIS AWARD!
BEST EVAH

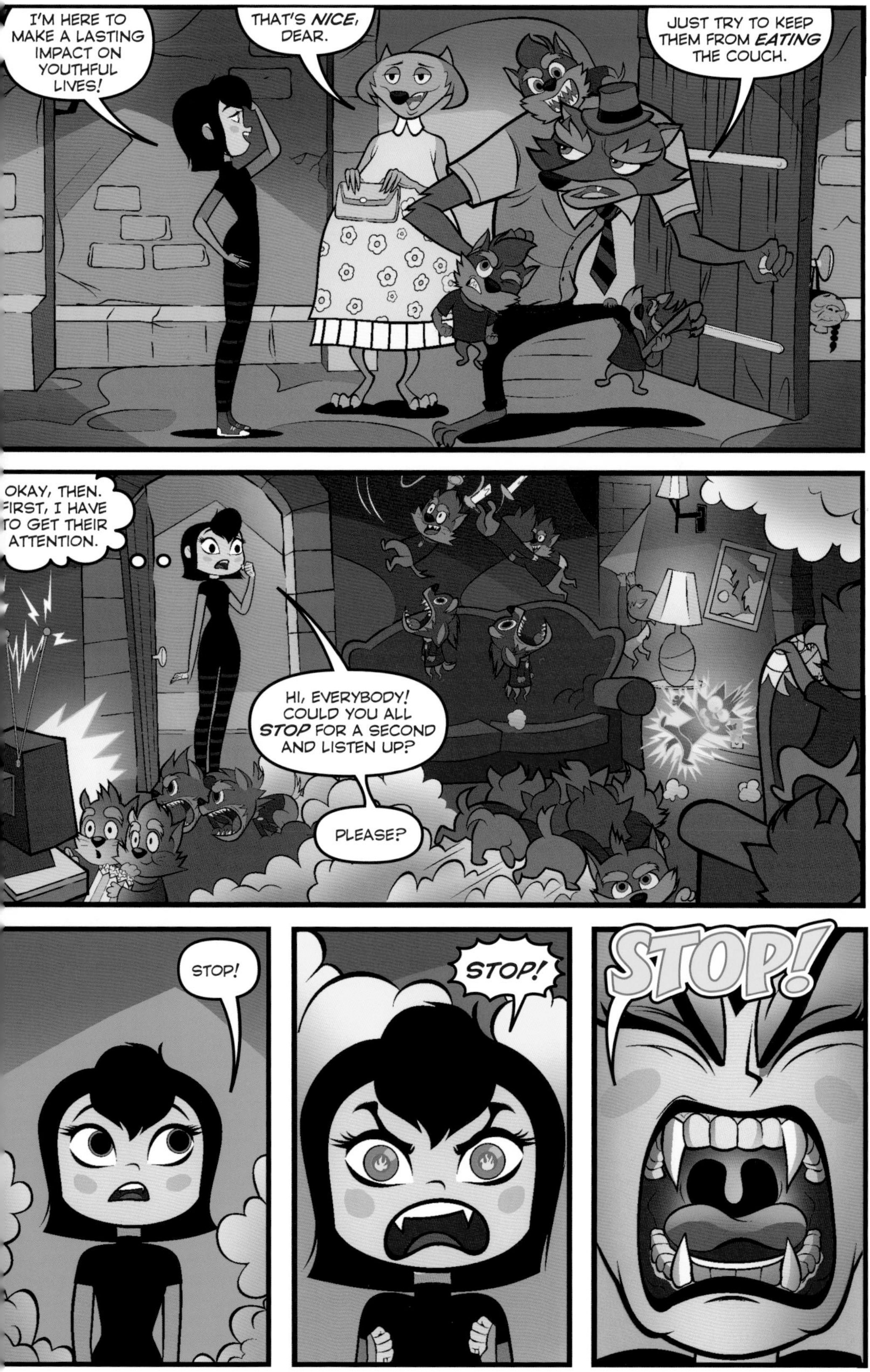
I'M HERE TO MAKE A LASTING IMPACT ON YOUTHFUL LIVES!
THAT'S NICE, DEAR.
JUST TRY TO KEEP THEM FROM EATING THE COUCH.
OKAY, THEN. FIRST, I HAVE TO GET THEIR ATTENTION.
HI, EVERYBODY! COULD YOU ALL STOP FOR A SECOND AND LISTEN UP?
PLEASE?
STOP!
STOP!
STOP!

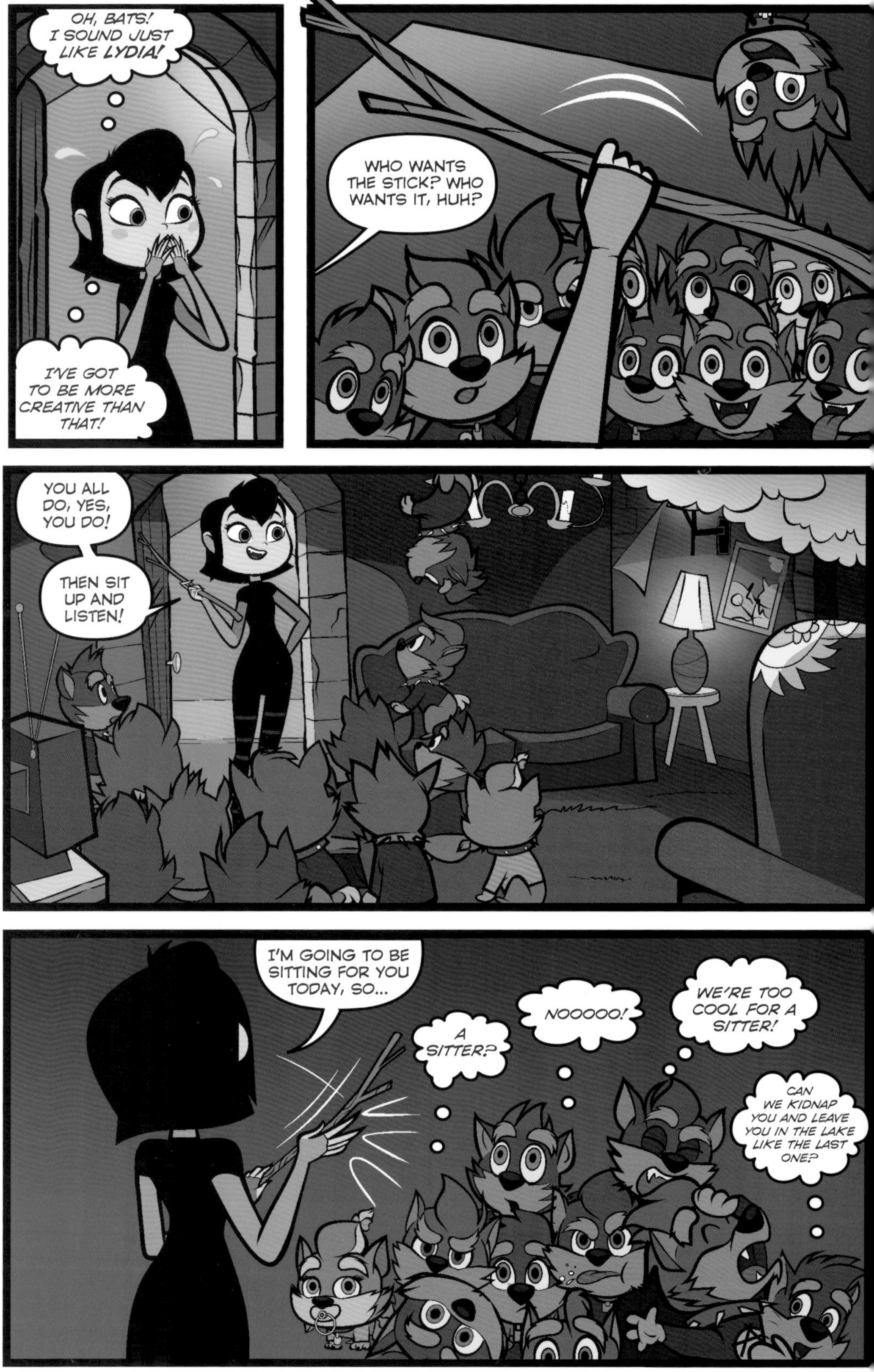
OH, BATS! I SOUND JUST LIKE LYDIA!
I'VE GOT TO BE MORE CREATIVE THAN THAT!
WHO WANTS THE STICK? WHO WANTS IT, HUH?
YOU ALL DO, YES, YOU DO!
THEN SIT UP AND LISTEN!
I'M GOING TO BE SITTING FOR YOU TODAY, SO...
A SITTER?
NOOOOO!
WE'RE TOO COOL FOR A SITTER!
CAN WE KIDNAP YOU AND LEAVE YOU IN THE LAKE LIKE THE LAST ONE?

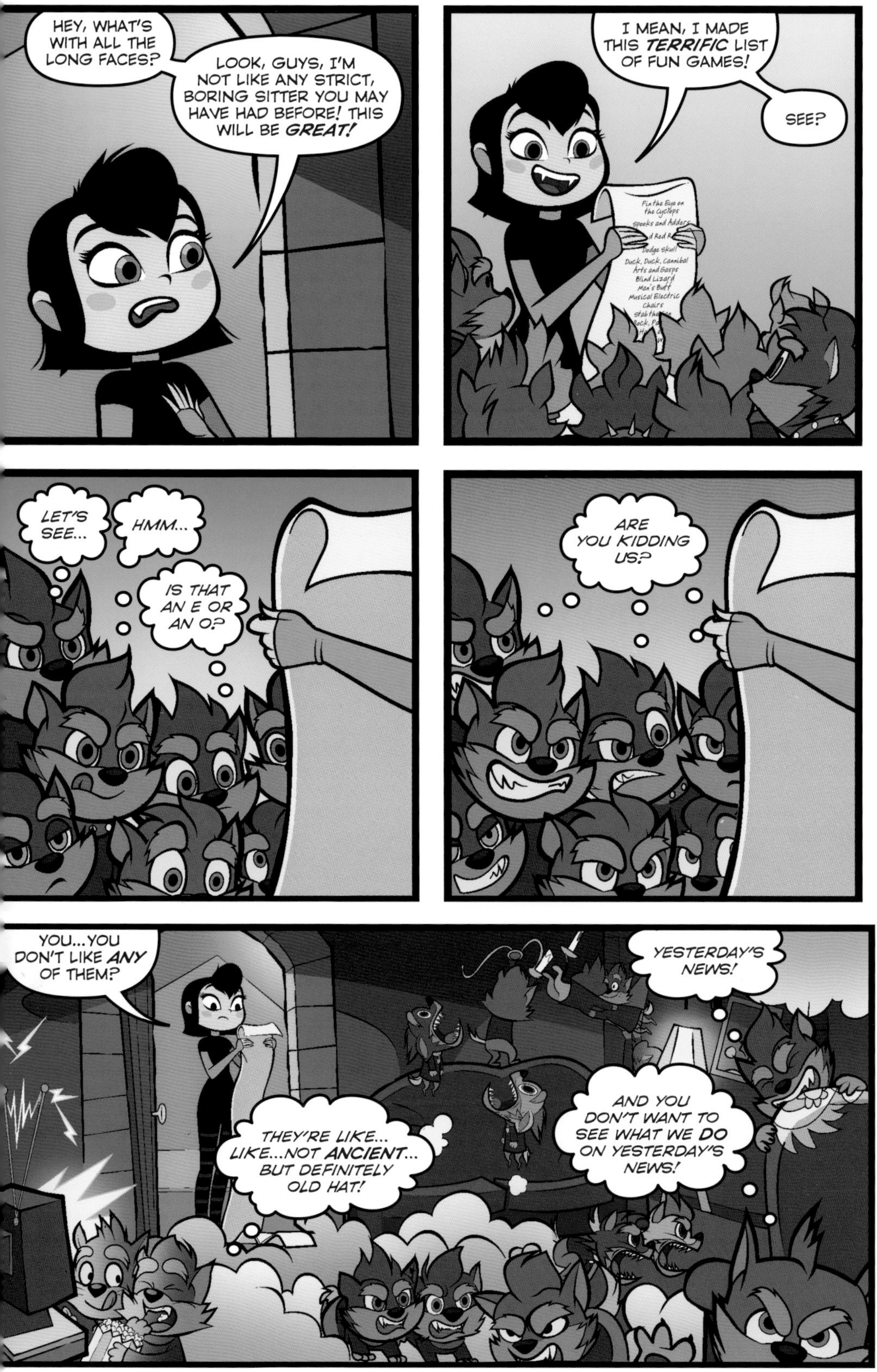
HEY, WHAT'S WITH ALL THE LONG FACES?
LOOK, GUYS, I'M NOT LIKE ANY STRICT, BORING SITTER YOU MAY HAVE HAD BEFORE! THIS WILL BE *GREAT!*
I MEAN, I MADE THIS *TERRIFIC* LIST OF FUN GAMES!
SEE?
Pin the Eye on the Cyclops
Spooks and Adders
Dodge Skull
Duck, Duck, Cannibal
Arts and Gasps
Blind Lizard
Man's Butt
Musical Electric Chairs
LET'S SEE...
HMM...
IS THAT AN E OR AN O?
ARE YOU KIDDING US?
YOU...YOU DON'T LIKE *ANY* OF THEM?
YESTERDAY'S NEWS!
THEY'RE LIKE... LIKE...NOT *ANCIENT*... BUT DEFINITELY OLD HAT!
AND YOU DON'T WANT TO SEE WHAT WE *DO* ON YESTERDAY'S NEWS!

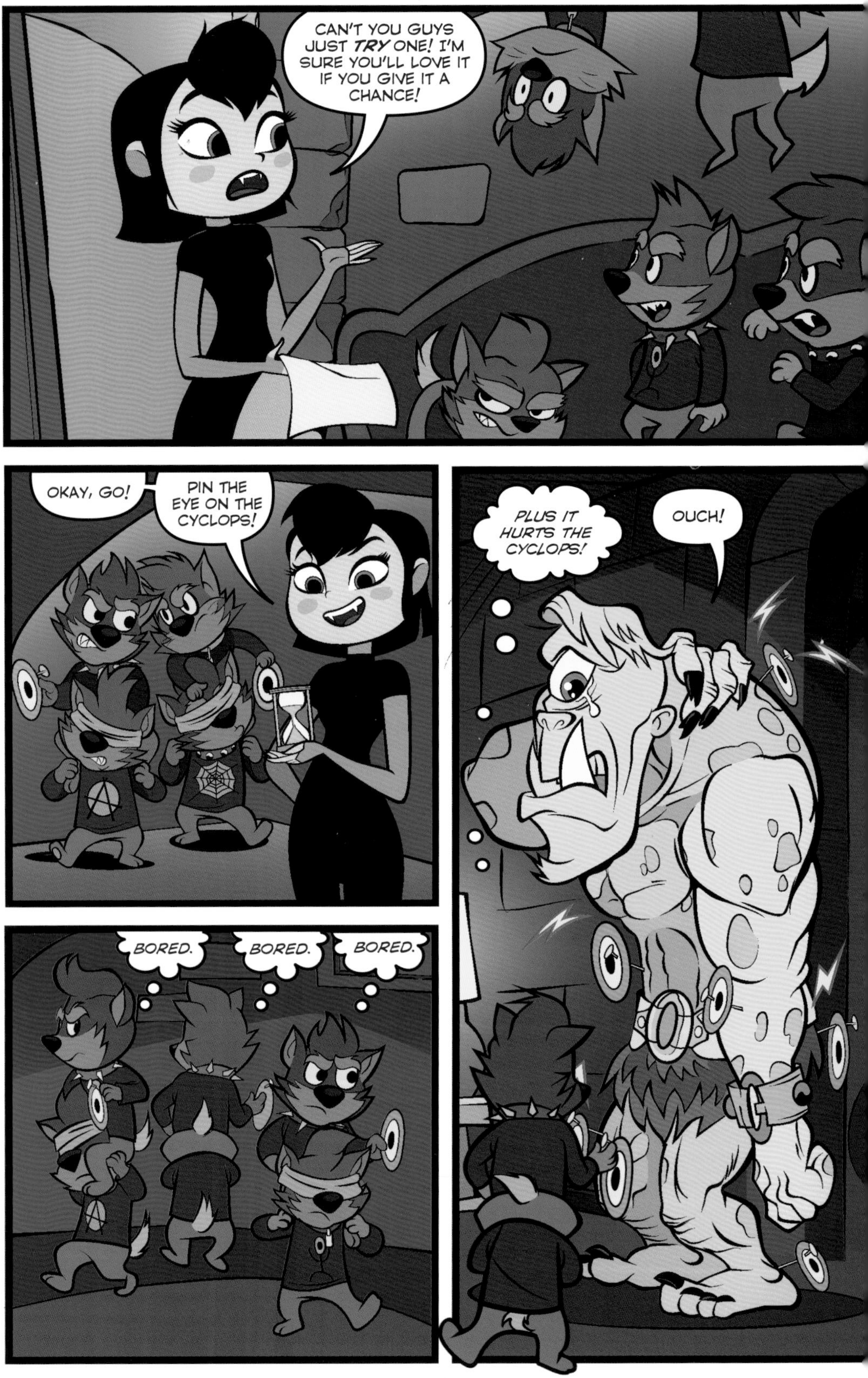
CAN'T YOU GUYS JUST *TRY* ONE! I'M SURE YOU'LL LOVE IT IF YOU GIVE IT A CHANCE!
OKAY, GO!
PIN THE EYE ON THE CYCLOPS!
BORED.
BORED.
BORED.
PLUS IT HURTS THE CYCLOPS!
OUCH!

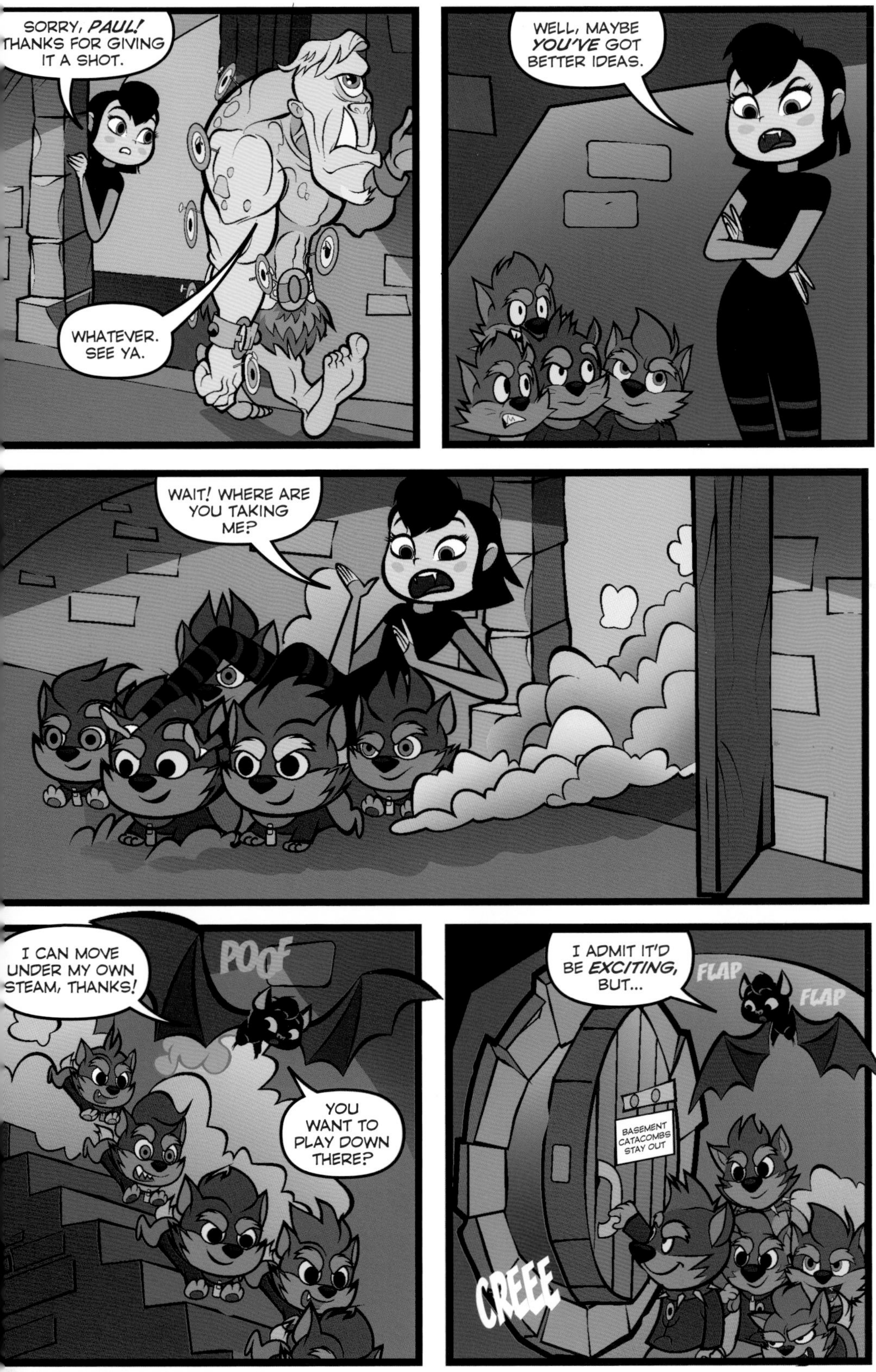
SORRY, *PAUL!* THANKS FOR GIVING IT A SHOT.
WHATEVER. SEE YA.
WELL, MAYBE *YOU'VE* GOT BETTER IDEAS.
WAIT! WHERE ARE YOU TAKING ME?
I CAN MOVE UNDER MY OWN STEAM, THANKS!
POOF
YOU WANT TO PLAY DOWN THERE?
I ADMIT IT'D BE *EXCITING*, BUT...
FLAP
FLAP
BASEMENT CATACOMBS STAY OUT
CREEE

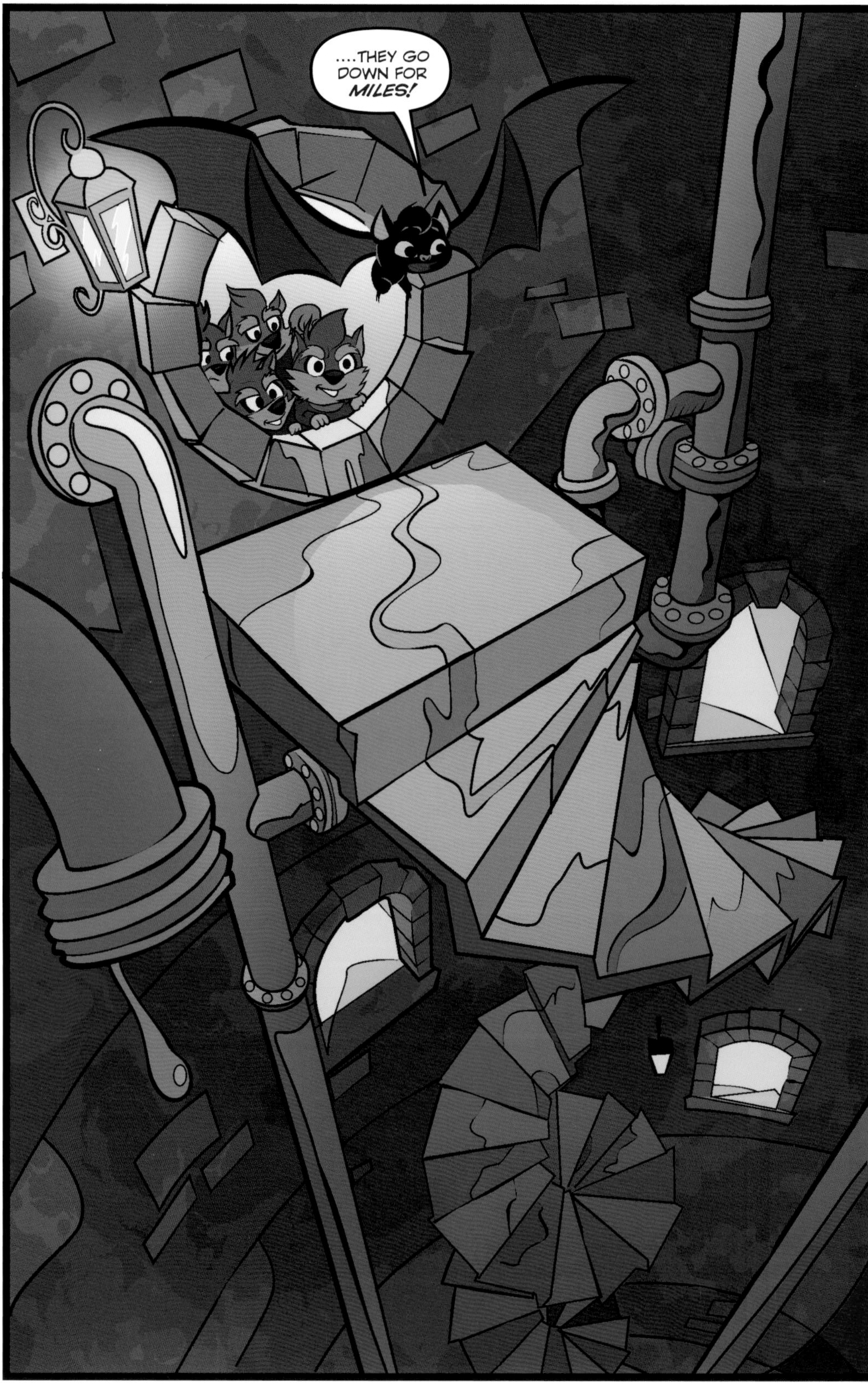
....THEY GO DOWN FOR *MILES!*

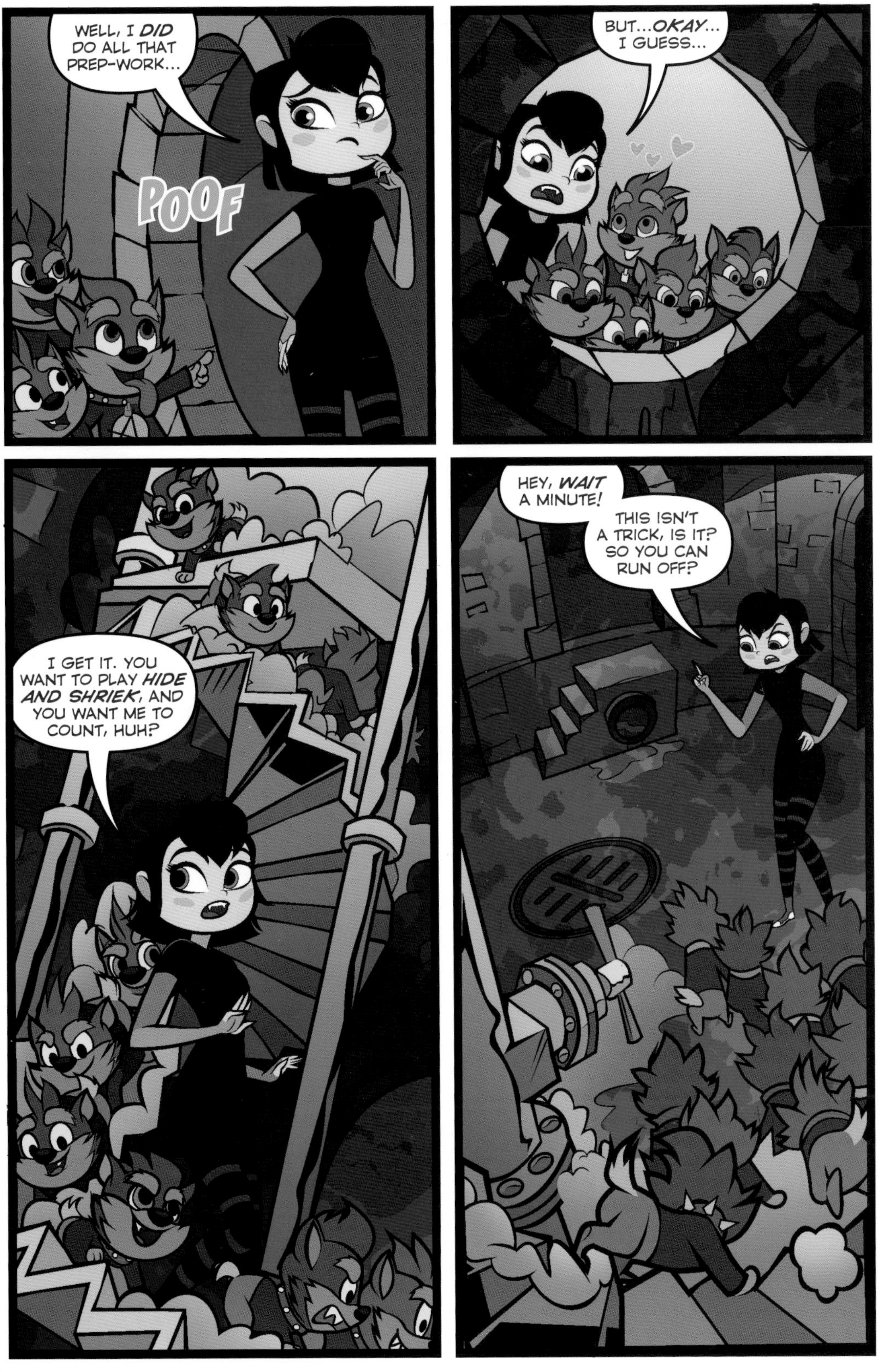
WELL, I *DID* DO ALL THAT PREP-WORK...
POOF
BUT...*OKAY*... I GUESS...
I GET IT. YOU WANT TO PLAY *HIDE AND SHRIEK*, AND YOU WANT ME TO COUNT, HUH?
HEY, *WAIT* A MINUTE!
THIS ISN'T A TRICK, IS IT? SO YOU CAN RUN OFF?

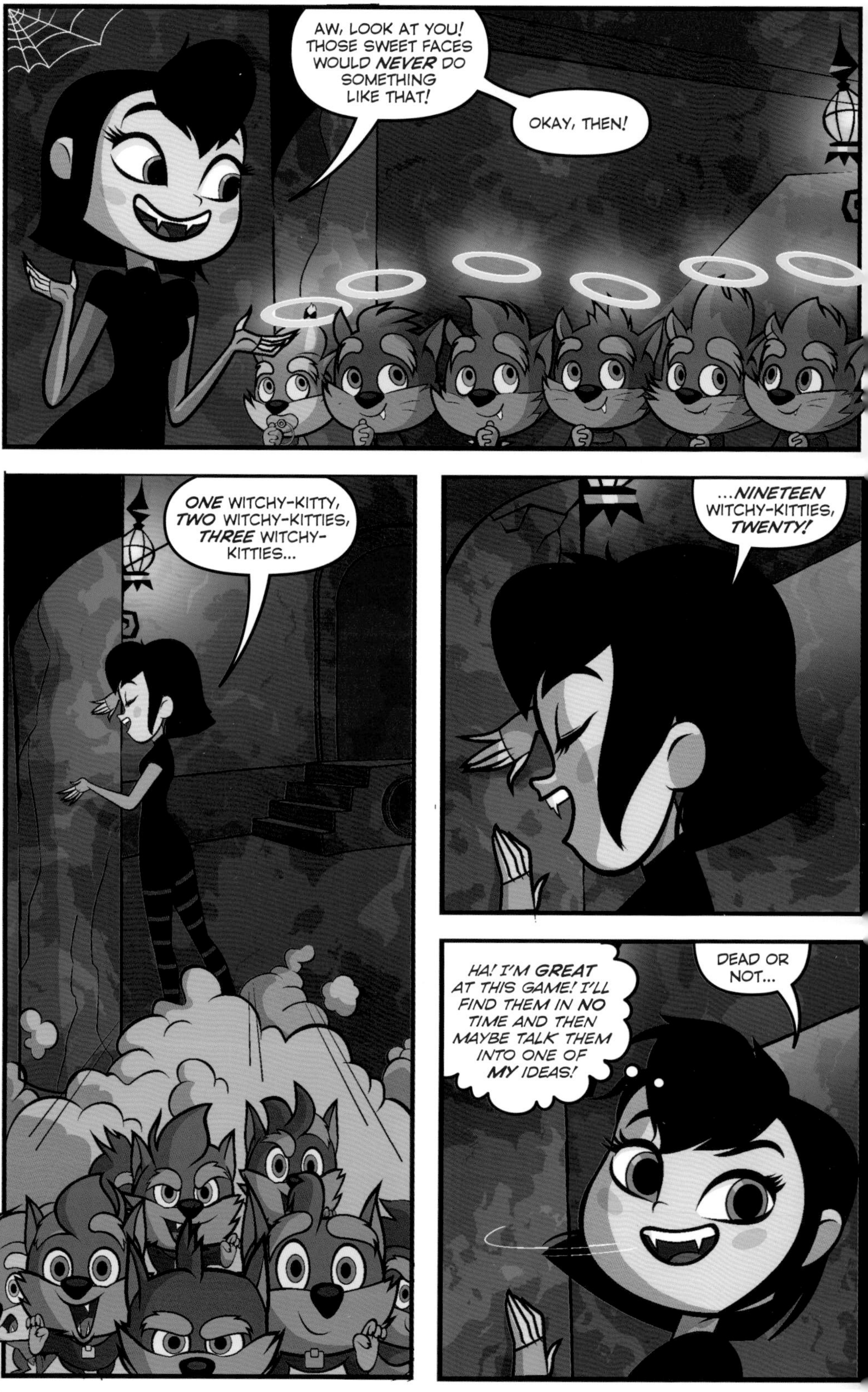
AW, LOOK AT YOU! THOSE SWEET FACES WOULD NEVER DO SOMETHING LIKE THAT!
OKAY, THEN!
ONE WITCHY-KITTY, TWO WITCHY-KITTIES, THREE WITCHY-KITTIES...
...NINETEEN WITCHY-KITTIES, TWENTY!
HA! I'M GREAT AT THIS GAME! I'LL FIND THEM IN NO TIME AND THEN MAYBE TALK THEM INTO ONE OF MY IDEAS!
DEAD OR NOT...

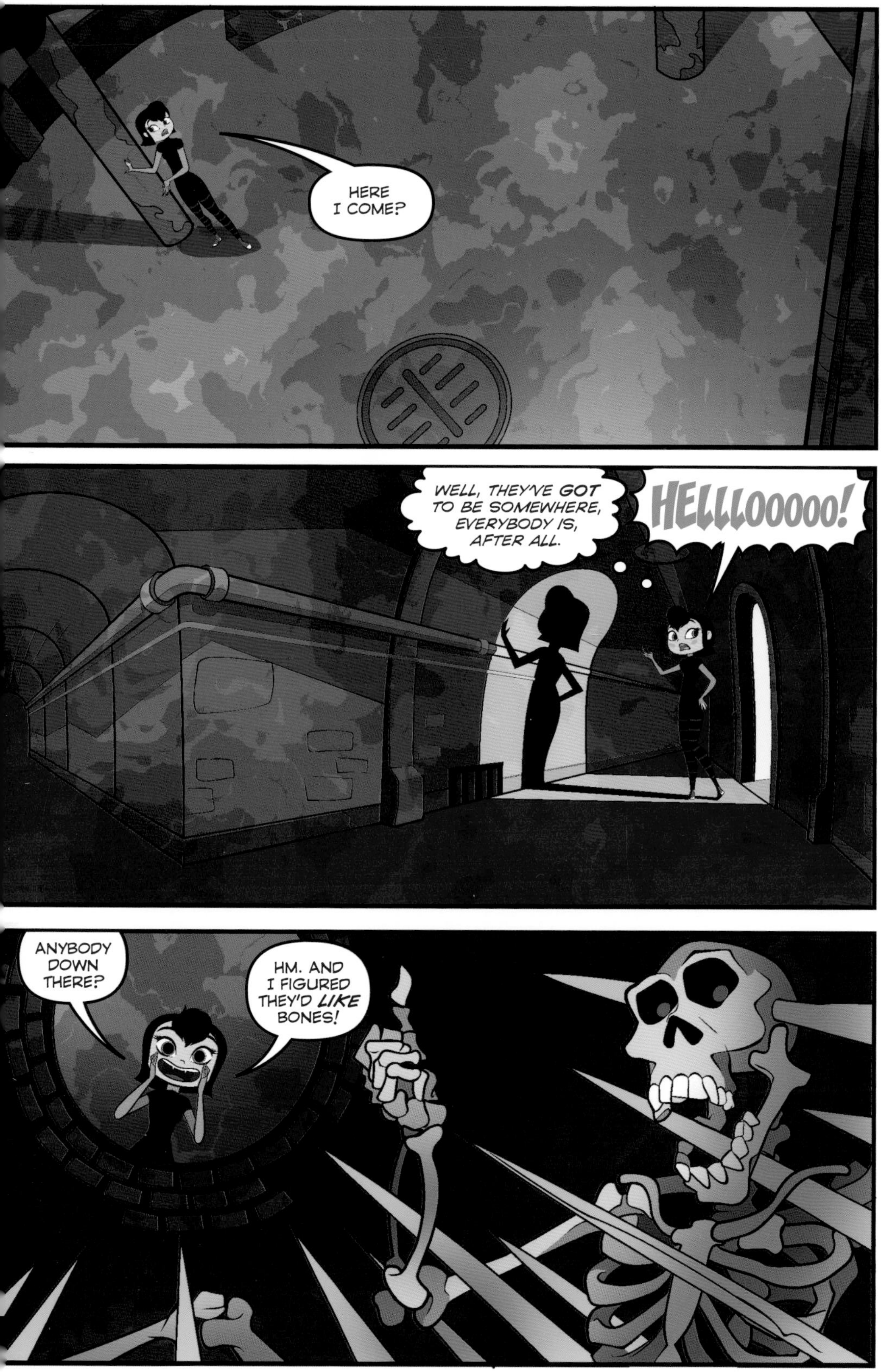
HERE I COME?
WELL, THEY'VE GOT TO BE SOMEWHERE, EVERYBODY IS, AFTER ALL.
HELLLOOOOO!
ANYBODY DOWN THERE?
HM. AND I FIGURED THEY'D LIKE BONES!

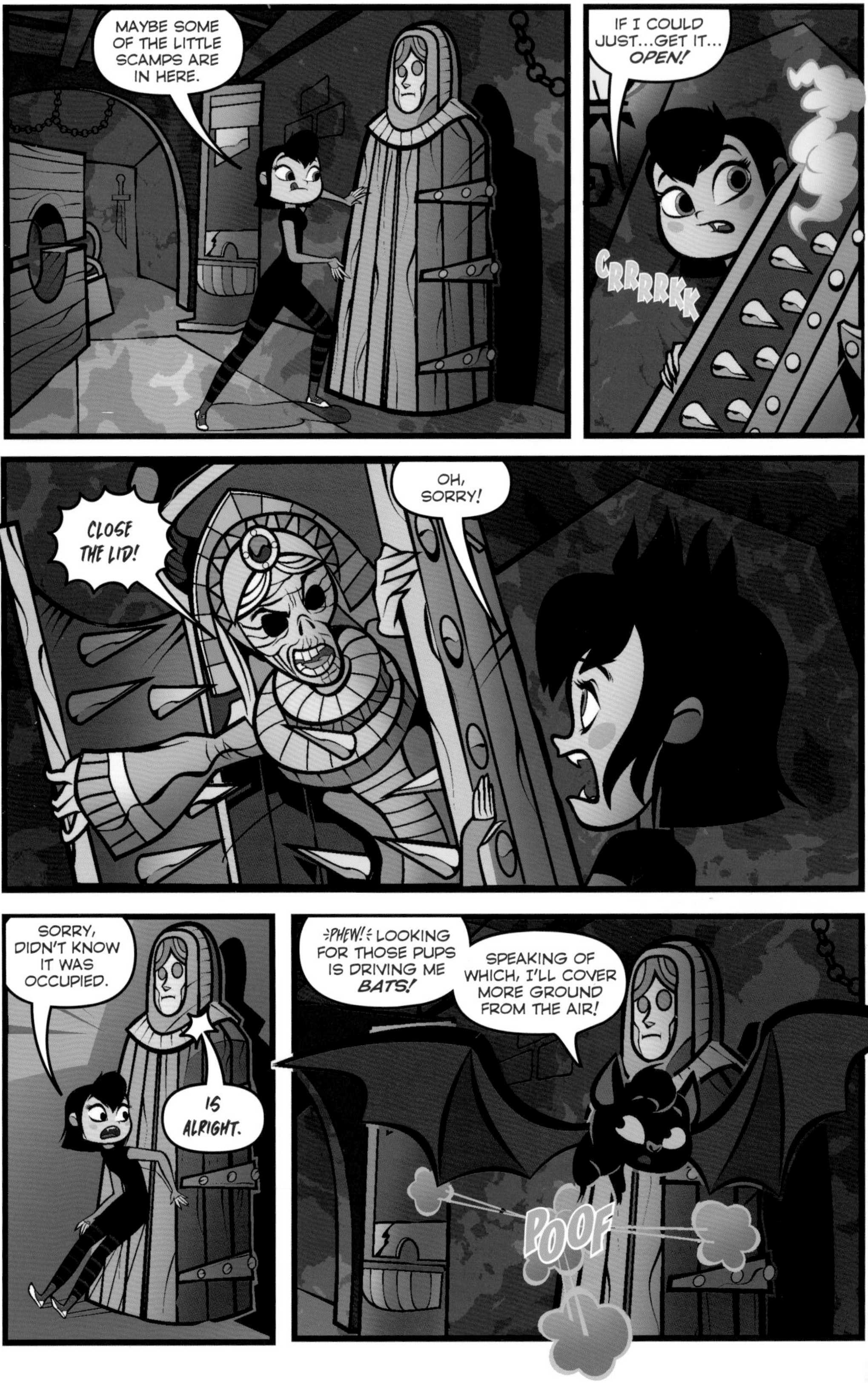
MAYBE SOME OF THE LITTLE SCAMPS ARE IN HERE.
IF I COULD JUST...GET IT... OPEN!
CRRRRKK
CLOSE THE LID!
OH, SORRY!
SORRY, DIDN'T KNOW IT WAS OCCUPIED.
IS ALRIGHT.
PHEW! LOOKING FOR THOSE PUPS IS DRIVING ME BATS!
SPEAKING OF WHICH, I'LL COVER MORE GROUND FROM THE AIR!
POOF

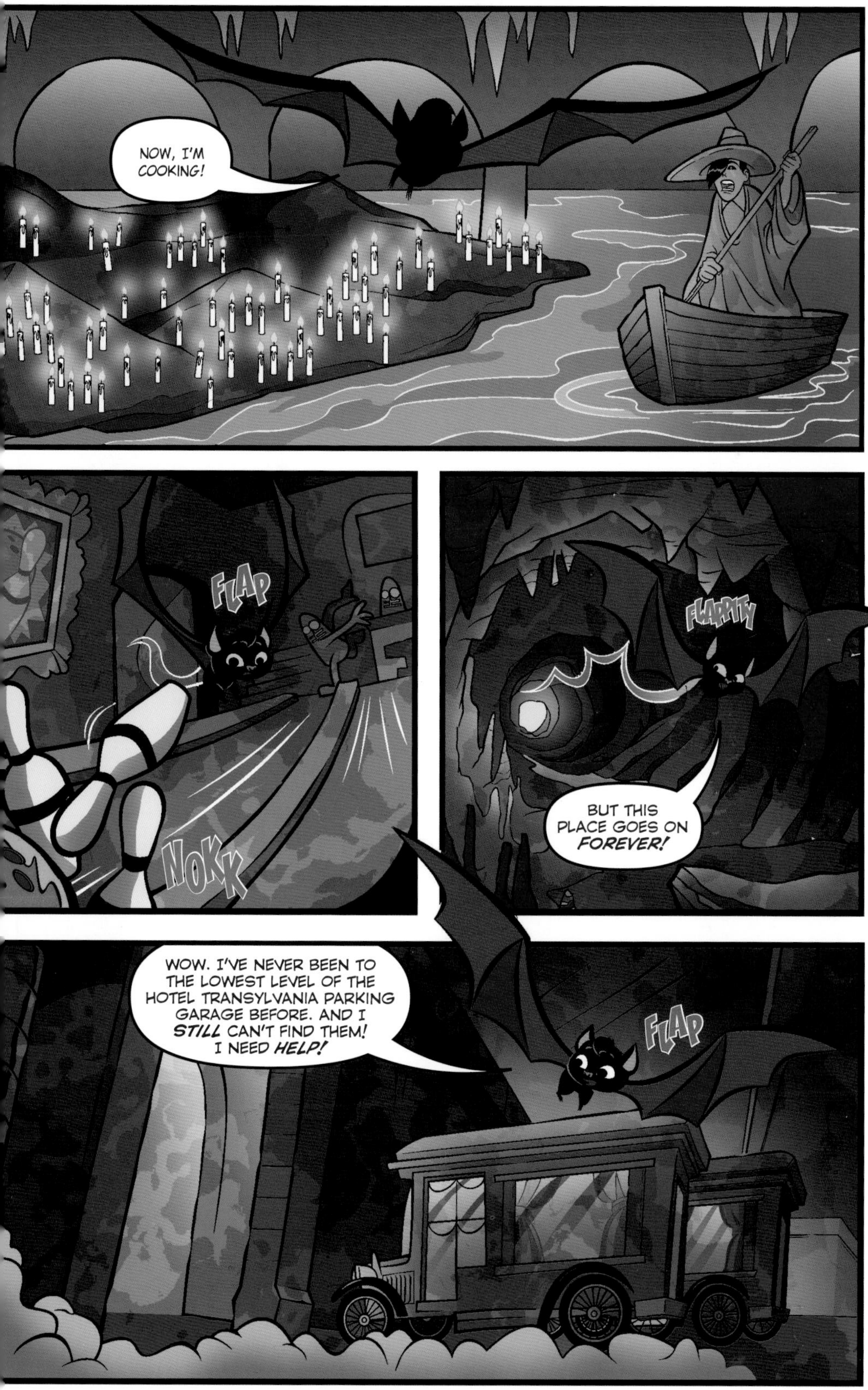
NOW, I'M COOKING!
FLAP
NOKK
FLAPPITY
BUT THIS PLACE GOES ON FOREVER!
WOW. I'VE NEVER BEEN TO THE LOWEST LEVEL OF THE HOTEL TRANSYLVANIA PARKING GARAGE BEFORE. AND I STILL CAN'T FIND THEM! I NEED HELP!
FLAP

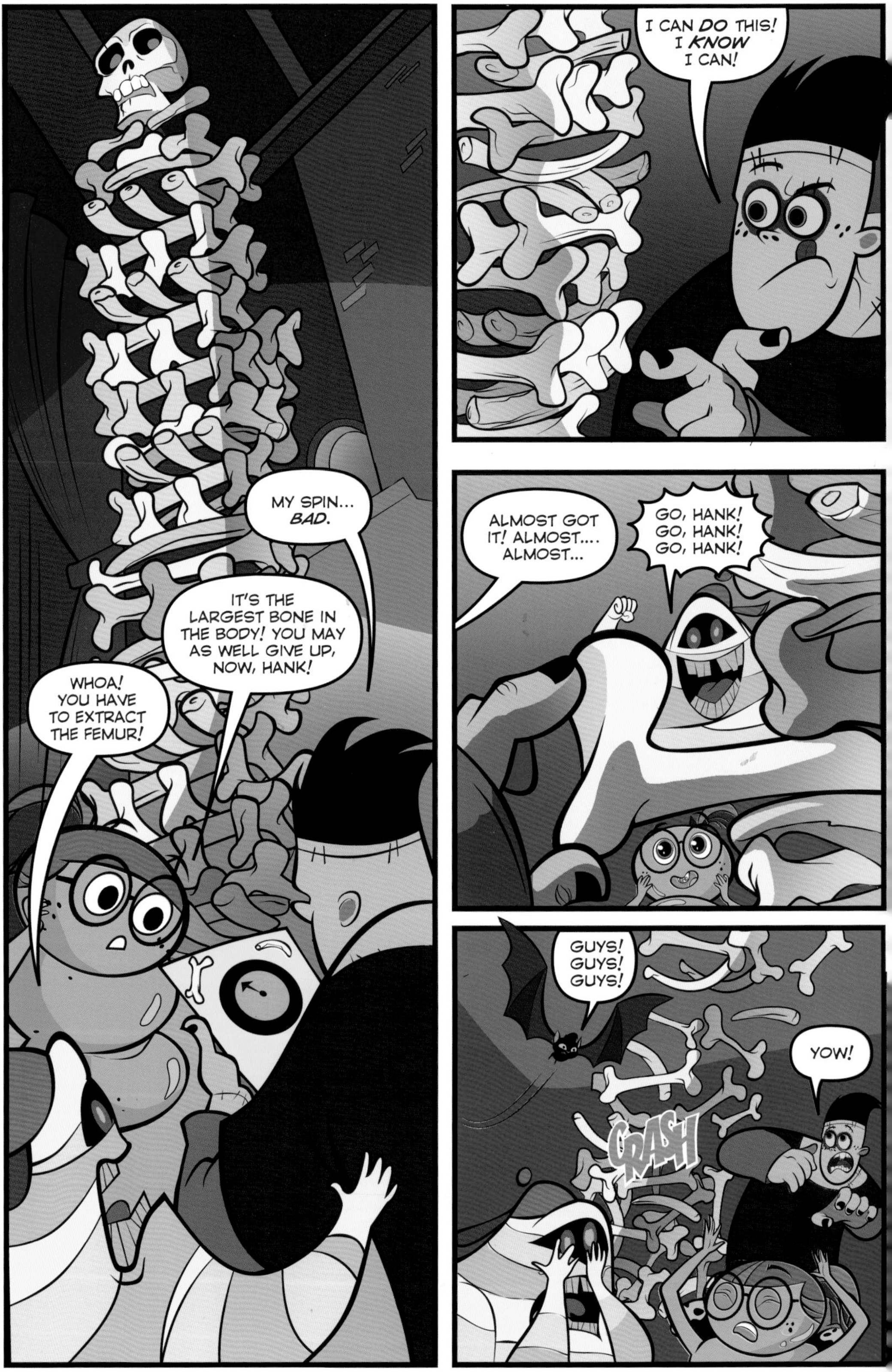
MY SPIN... BAD.
IT'S THE LARGEST BONE IN THE BODY! YOU MAY AS WELL GIVE UP, NOW, HANK!
WHOA! YOU HAVE TO EXTRACT THE FEMUR!
I CAN DO THIS! I KNOW I CAN!
ALMOST GOT IT! ALMOST.... ALMOST...
GO, HANK! GO, HANK! GO, HANK!
GUYS! GUYS! GUYS!
YOW!
CRASH

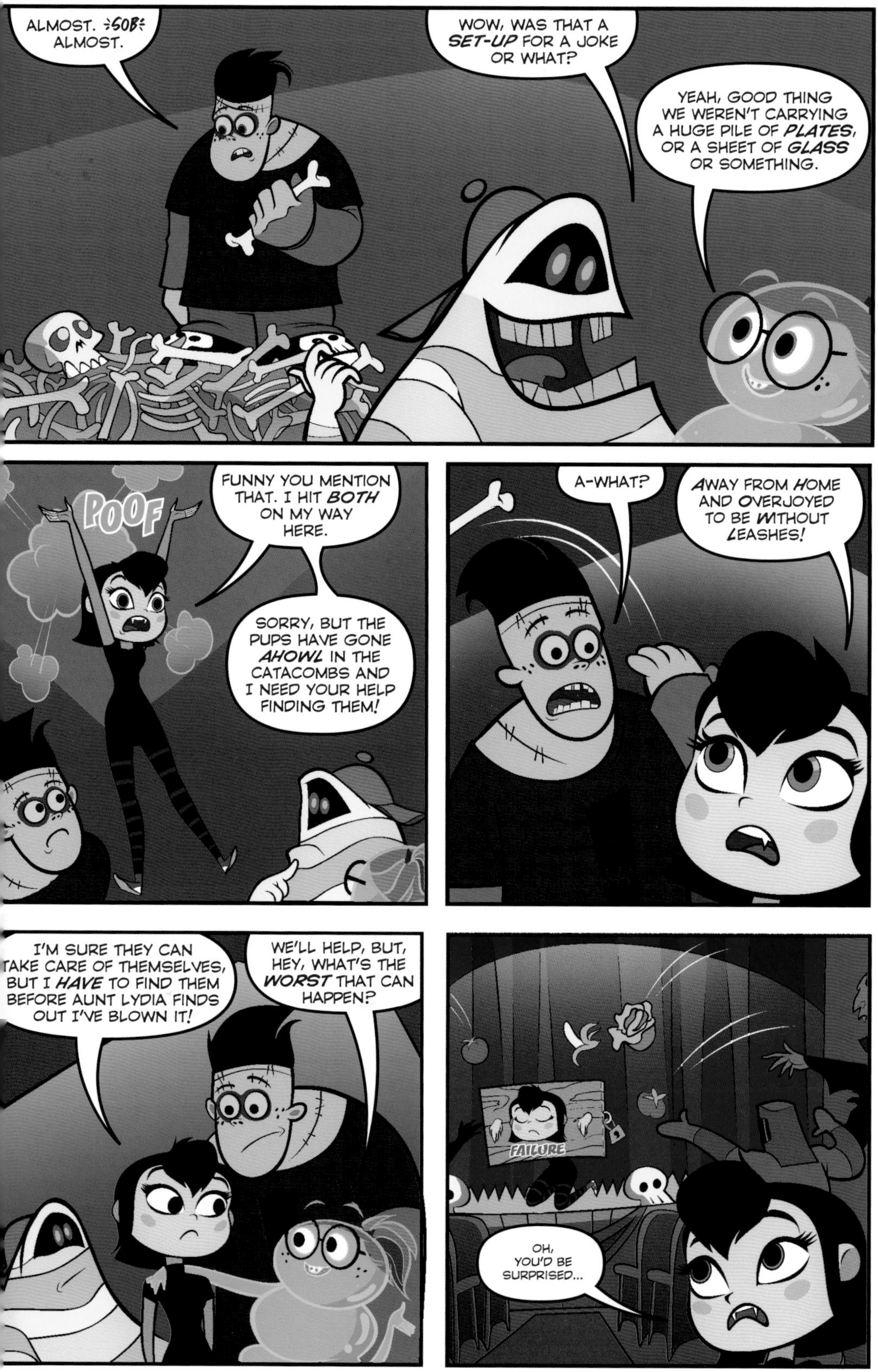
ALMOST. ⁑SOB⁑ ALMOST.
WOW, WAS THAT A SET-UP FOR A JOKE OR WHAT?
YEAH, GOOD THING WE WEREN'T CARRYING A HUGE PILE OF PLATES, OR A SHEET OF GLASS OR SOMETHING.
POOF
FUNNY YOU MENTION THAT. I HIT BOTH ON MY WAY HERE.
SORRY, BUT THE PUPS HAVE GONE AHOWL IN THE CATACOMBS AND I NEED YOUR HELP FINDING THEM!
A-WHAT?
AWAY FROM HOME AND OVERJOYED TO BE WITHOUT LEASHES!
I'M SURE THEY CAN TAKE CARE OF THEMSELVES, BUT I HAVE TO FIND THEM BEFORE AUNT LYDIA FINDS OUT I'VE BLOWN IT!
WE'LL HELP, BUT, HEY, WHAT'S THE WORST THAT CAN HAPPEN?
FAILURE
OH, YOU'D BE SURPRISED...

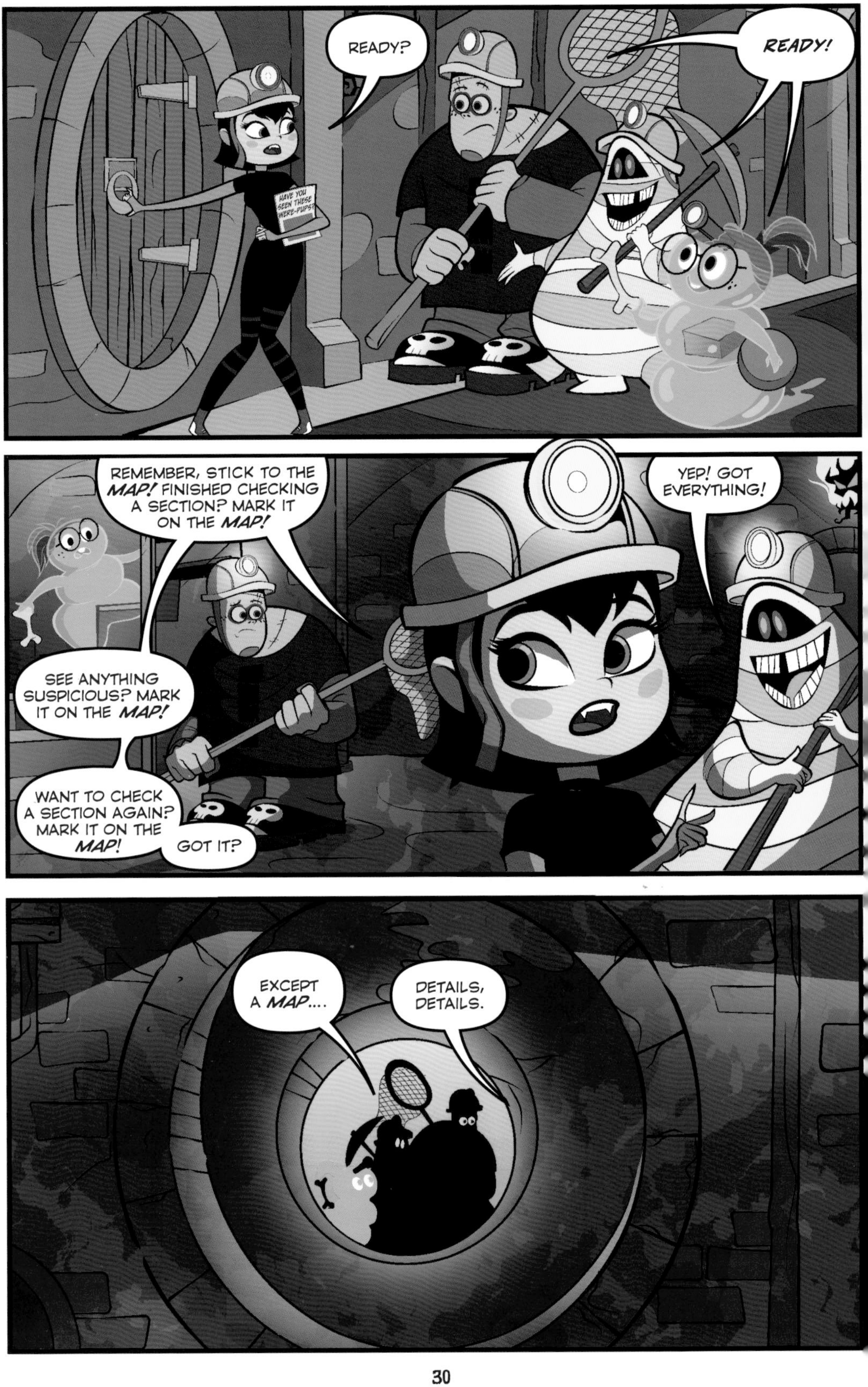
READY?
READY!
HAVE YOU SEEN THESE WERE-PUPS?
REMEMBER, STICK TO THE MAP! FINISHED CHECKING A SECTION? MARK IT ON THE MAP!
SEE ANYTHING SUSPICIOUS? MARK IT ON THE MAP!
WANT TO CHECK A SECTION AGAIN? MARK IT ON THE MAP!
GOT IT?
YEP! GOT EVERYTHING!
EXCEPT A MAP....
DETAILS, DETAILS.

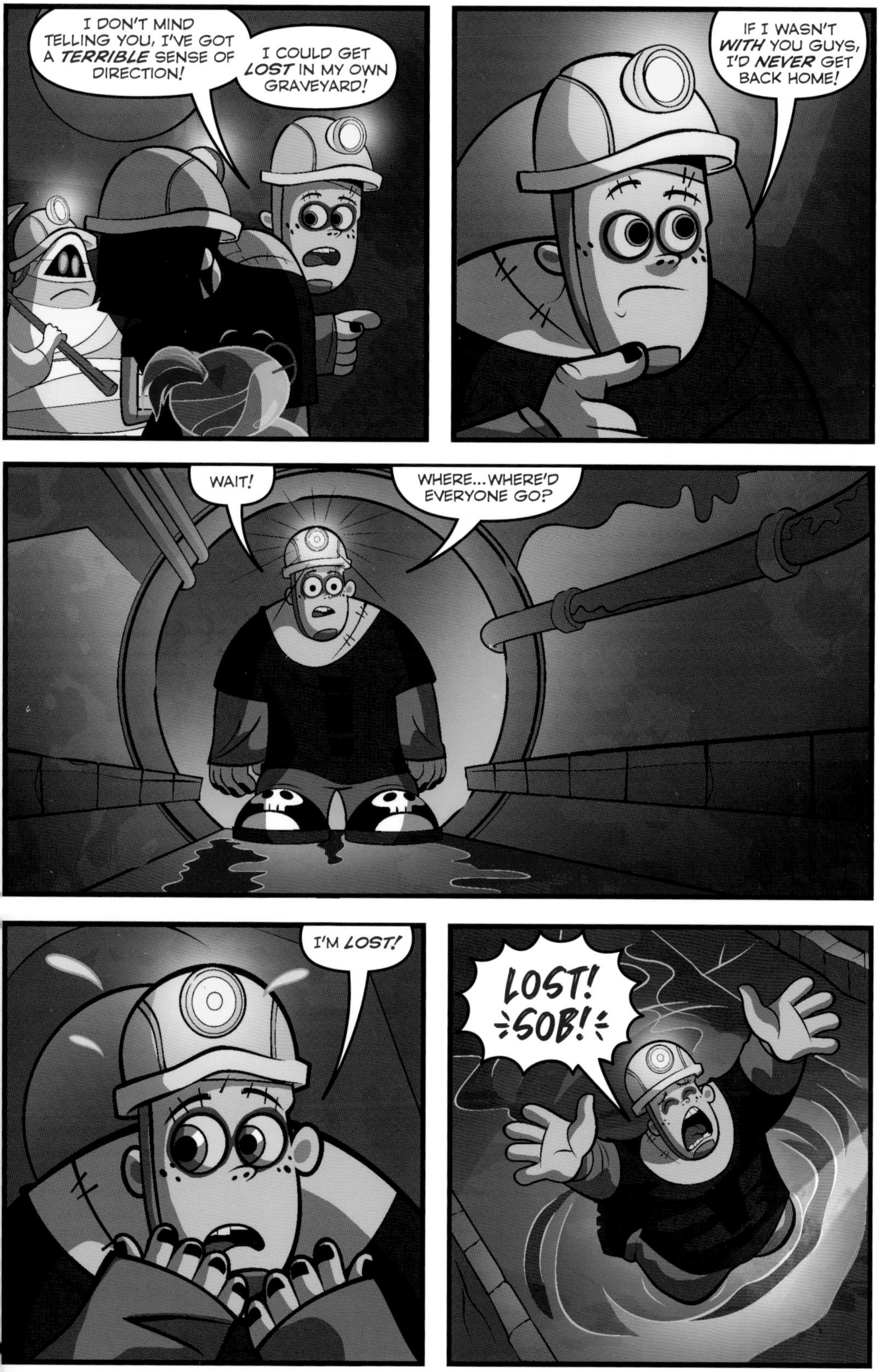
I DON'T MIND TELLING YOU, I'VE GOT A TERRIBLE SENSE OF DIRECTION!
I COULD GET LOST IN MY OWN GRAVEYARD!
IF I WASN'T WITH YOU GUYS, I'D NEVER GET BACK HOME!
WAIT!
WHERE...WHERE'D EVERYONE GO?
I'M LOST!
LOST! SOB!

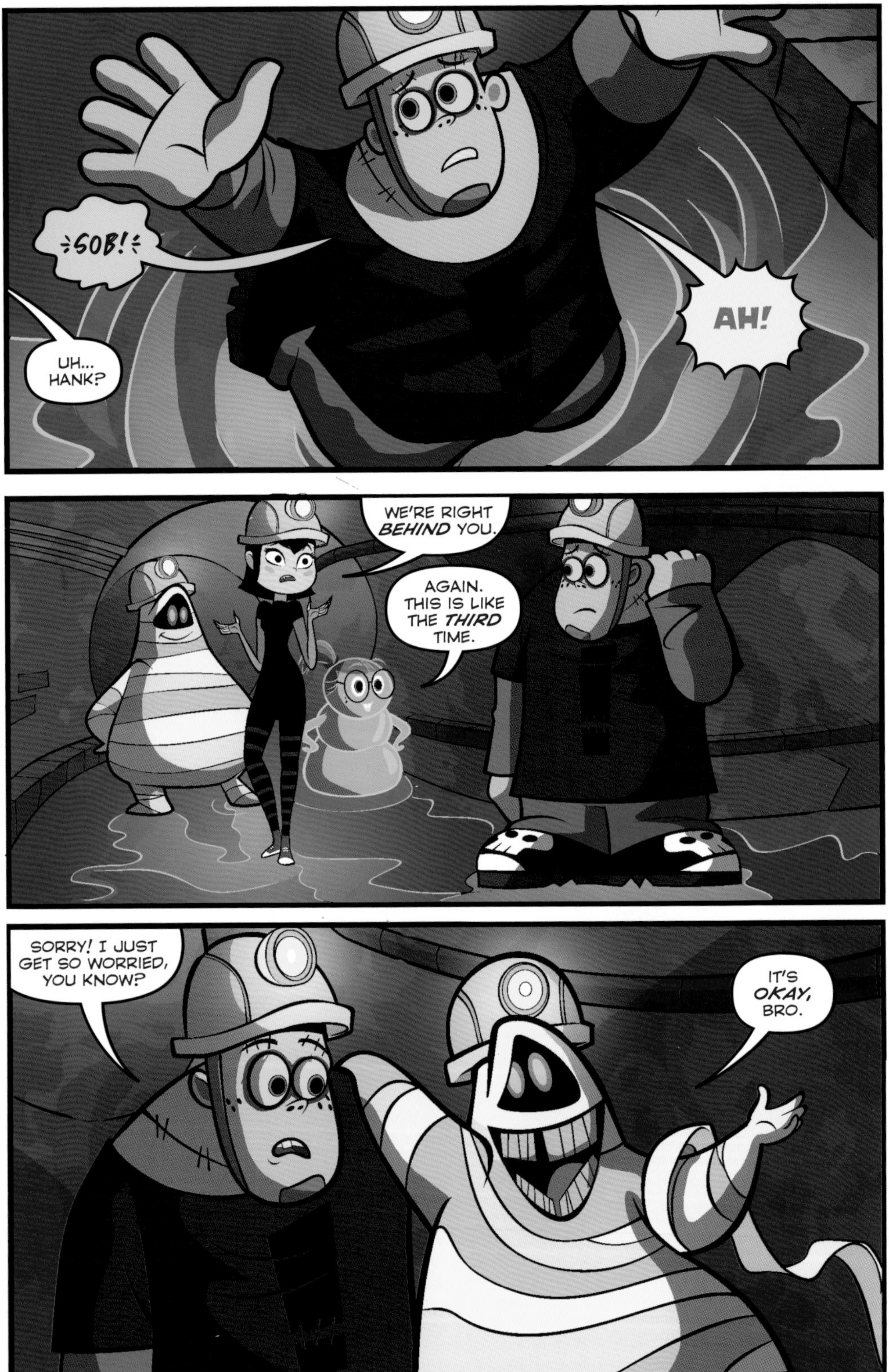
SOB!
AH!
UH... HANK?
WE'RE RIGHT *BEHIND* YOU.
AGAIN. THIS IS LIKE THE *THIRD* TIME.
SORRY! I JUST GET SO WORRIED, YOU KNOW?
IT'S *OKAY,* BRO.

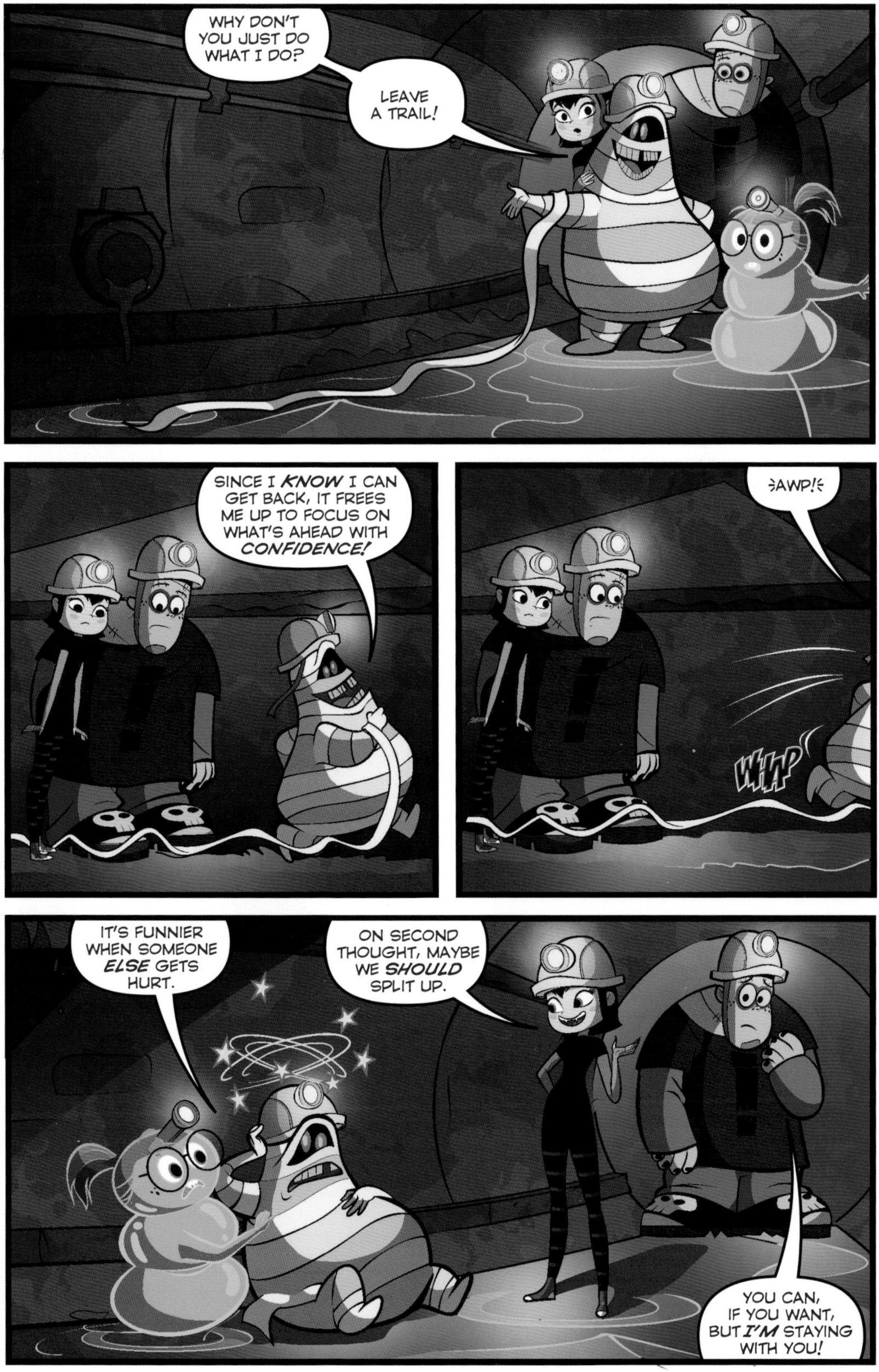
WHY DON'T YOU JUST DO WHAT I DO?
LEAVE A TRAIL!
SINCE I KNOW I CAN GET BACK, IT FREES ME UP TO FOCUS ON WHAT'S AHEAD WITH CONFIDENCE!
AWP!
WHAP
IT'S FUNNIER WHEN SOMEONE ELSE GETS HURT.
ON SECOND THOUGHT, MAYBE WE SHOULD SPLIT UP.
YOU CAN, IF YOU WANT, BUT I'M STAYING WITH YOU!

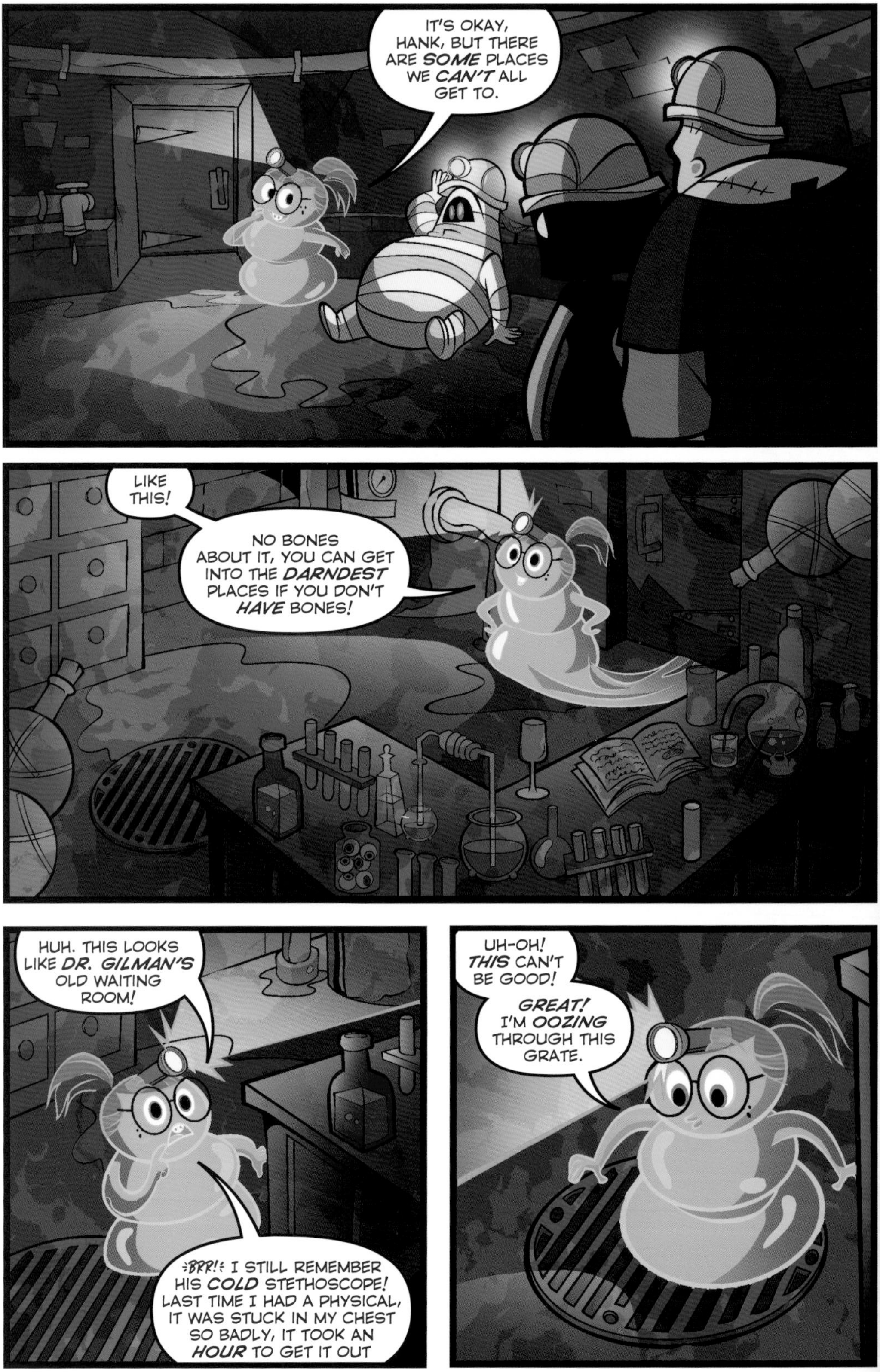
IT'S OKAY, HANK, BUT THERE ARE SOME PLACES WE CAN'T ALL GET TO.
LIKE THIS!
NO BONES ABOUT IT, YOU CAN GET INTO THE DARNDEST PLACES IF YOU DON'T HAVE BONES!
HUH. THIS LOOKS LIKE DR. GILMAN'S OLD WAITING ROOM!
BRR! I STILL REMEMBER HIS COLD STETHOSCOPE! LAST TIME I HAD A PHYSICAL, IT WAS STUCK IN MY CHEST SO BADLY, IT TOOK AN HOUR TO GET IT OUT
UH-OH! THIS CAN'T BE GOOD!
GREAT! I'M OOZING THROUGH THIS GRATE.

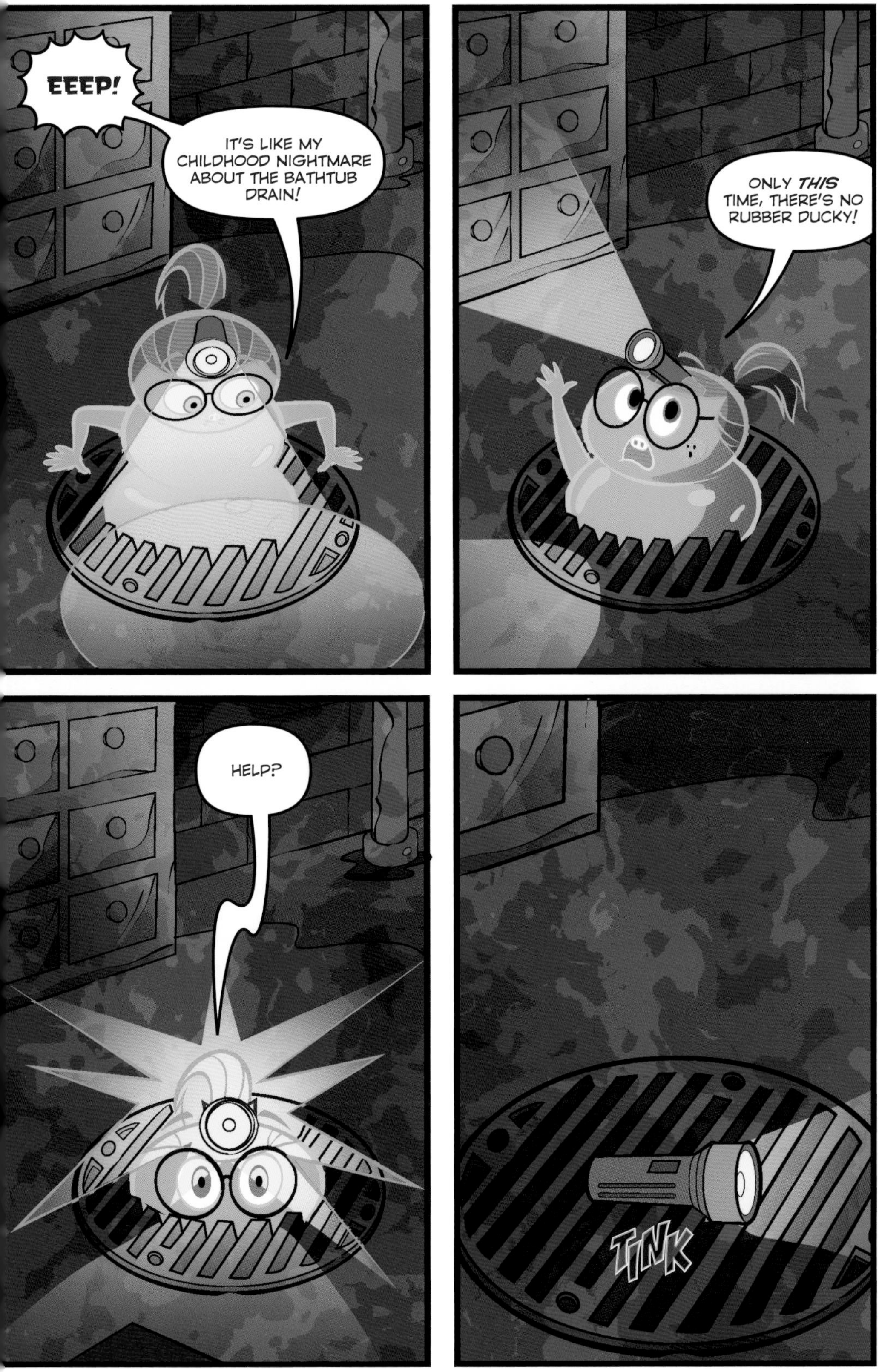
EEEP!
IT'S LIKE MY CHILDHOOD NIGHTMARE ABOUT THE BATHTUB DRAIN!
ONLY *THIS* TIME, THERE'S NO RUBBER DUCKY!
HELP?
TINK

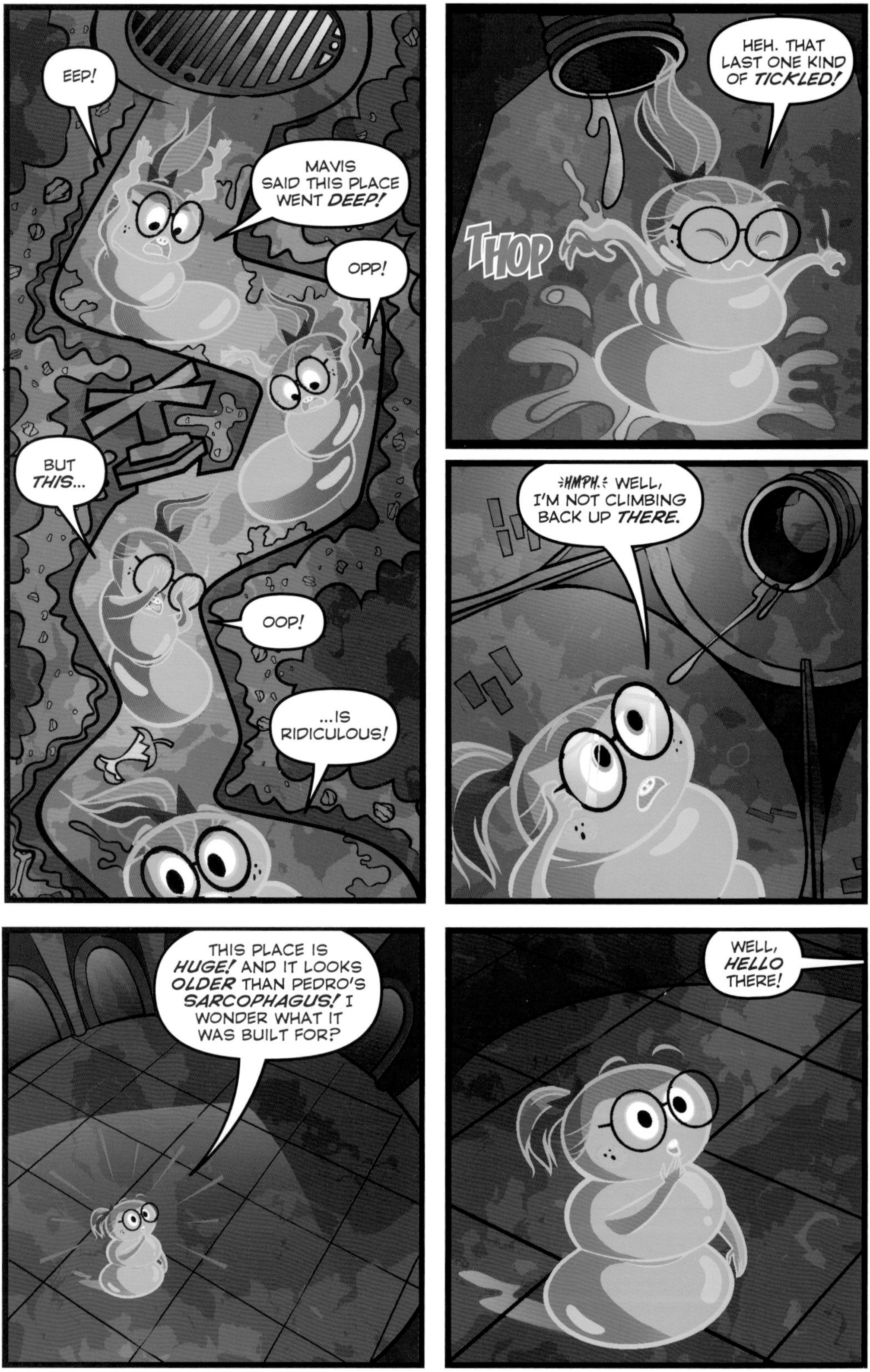
EEP!
MAVIS SAID THIS PLACE WENT DEEP!
OPP!
BUT THIS...
OOP!
...IS RIDICULOUS!
HEH. THAT LAST ONE KIND OF TICKLED!
THOP
HMPH. WELL, I'M NOT CLIMBING BACK UP THERE.
THIS PLACE IS HUGE! AND IT LOOKS OLDER THAN PEDRO'S SARCOPHAGUS! I WONDER WHAT IT WAS BUILT FOR?
WELL, HELLO THERE!

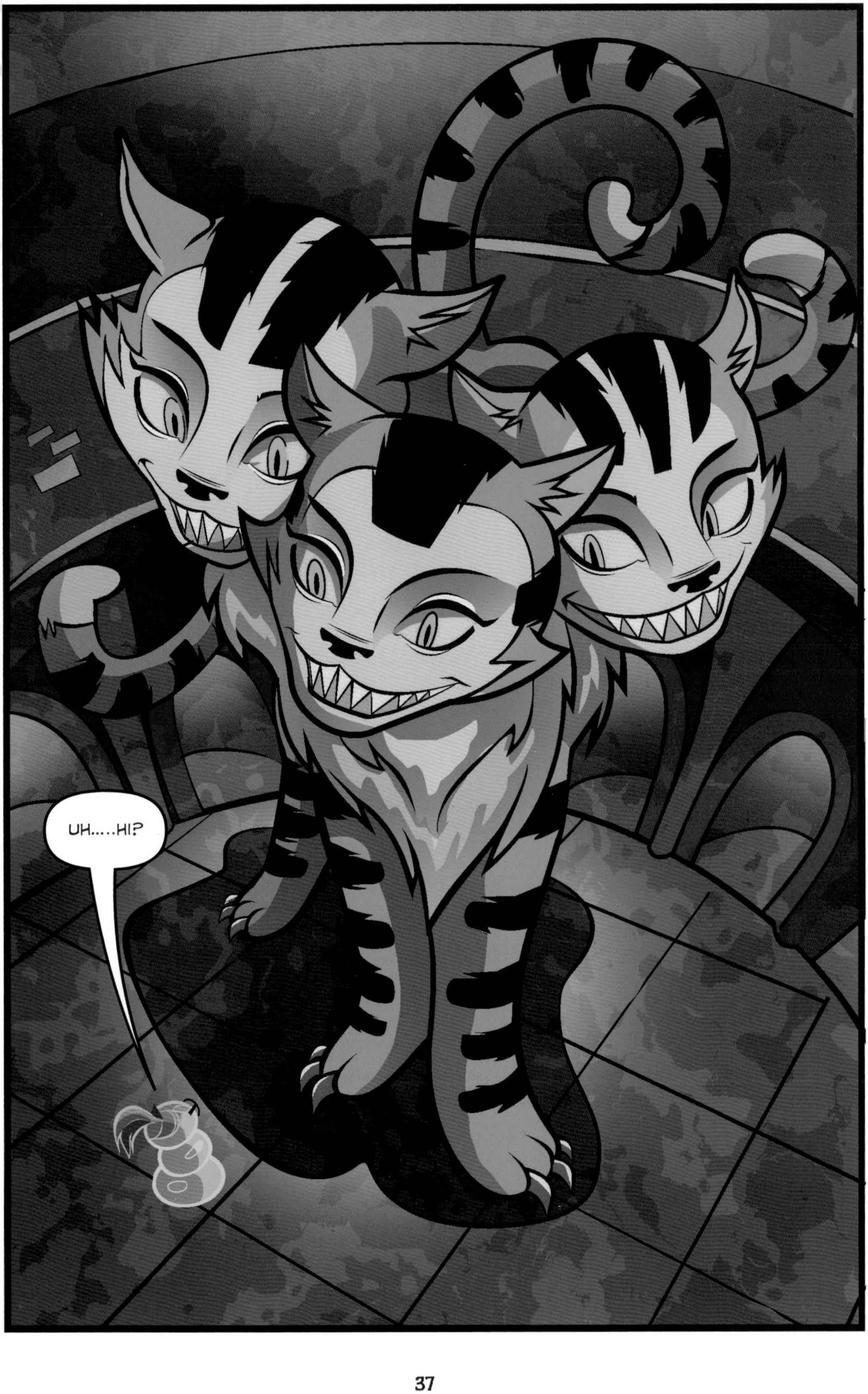
UH.....HI?

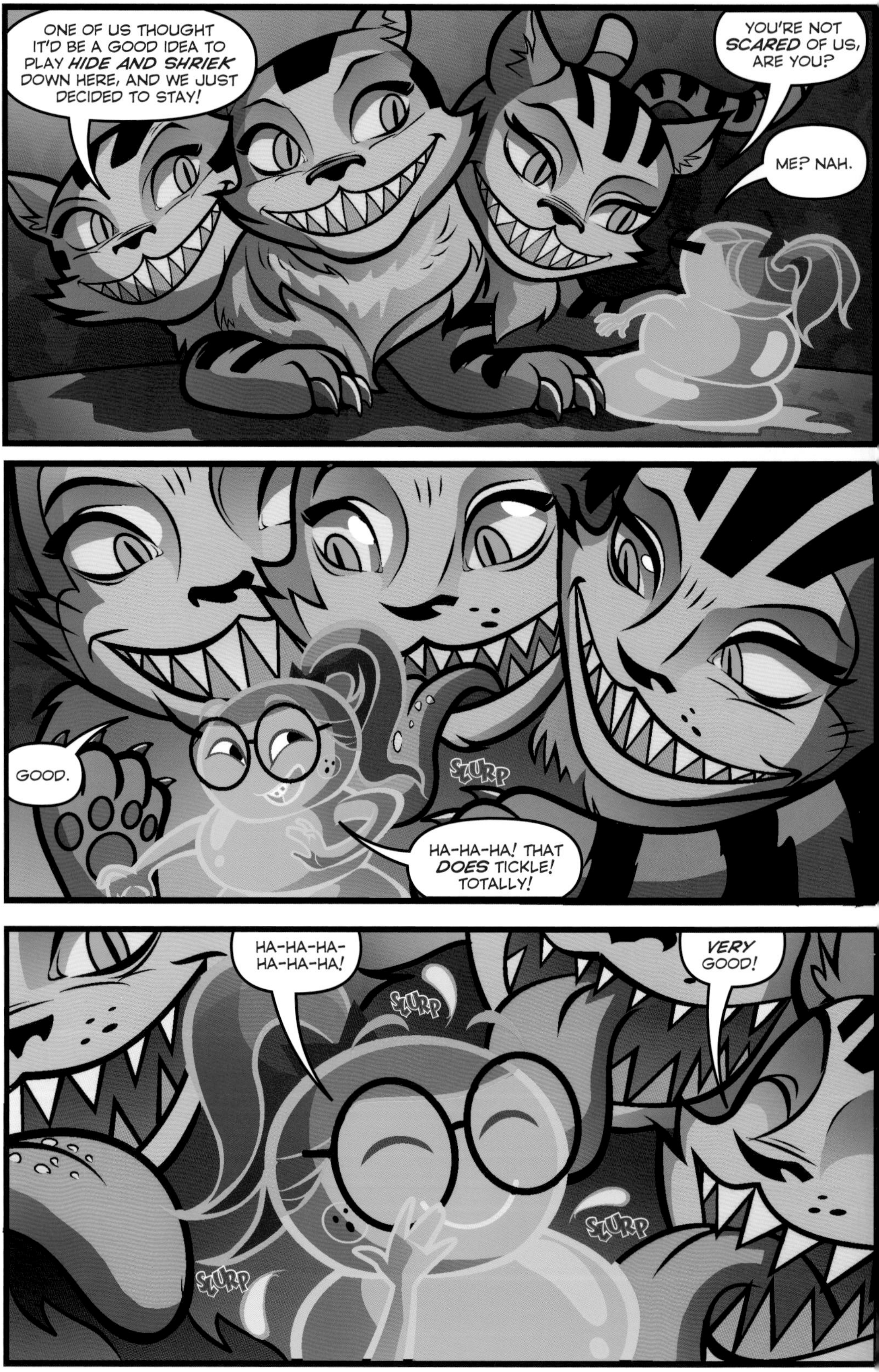

ONE OF US THOUGHT IT'D BE A GOOD IDEA TO PLAY *HIDE AND SHRIEK* DOWN HERE, AND WE JUST DECIDED TO STAY!
YOU'RE NOT *SCARED* OF US, ARE YOU?
ME? NAH.
GOOD.
SLURP
HA-HA-HA! THAT *DOES* TICKLE! TOTALLY!
HA-HA-HA-HA-HA-HA!
VERY GOOD!
SLURP
SLURP
SLURP

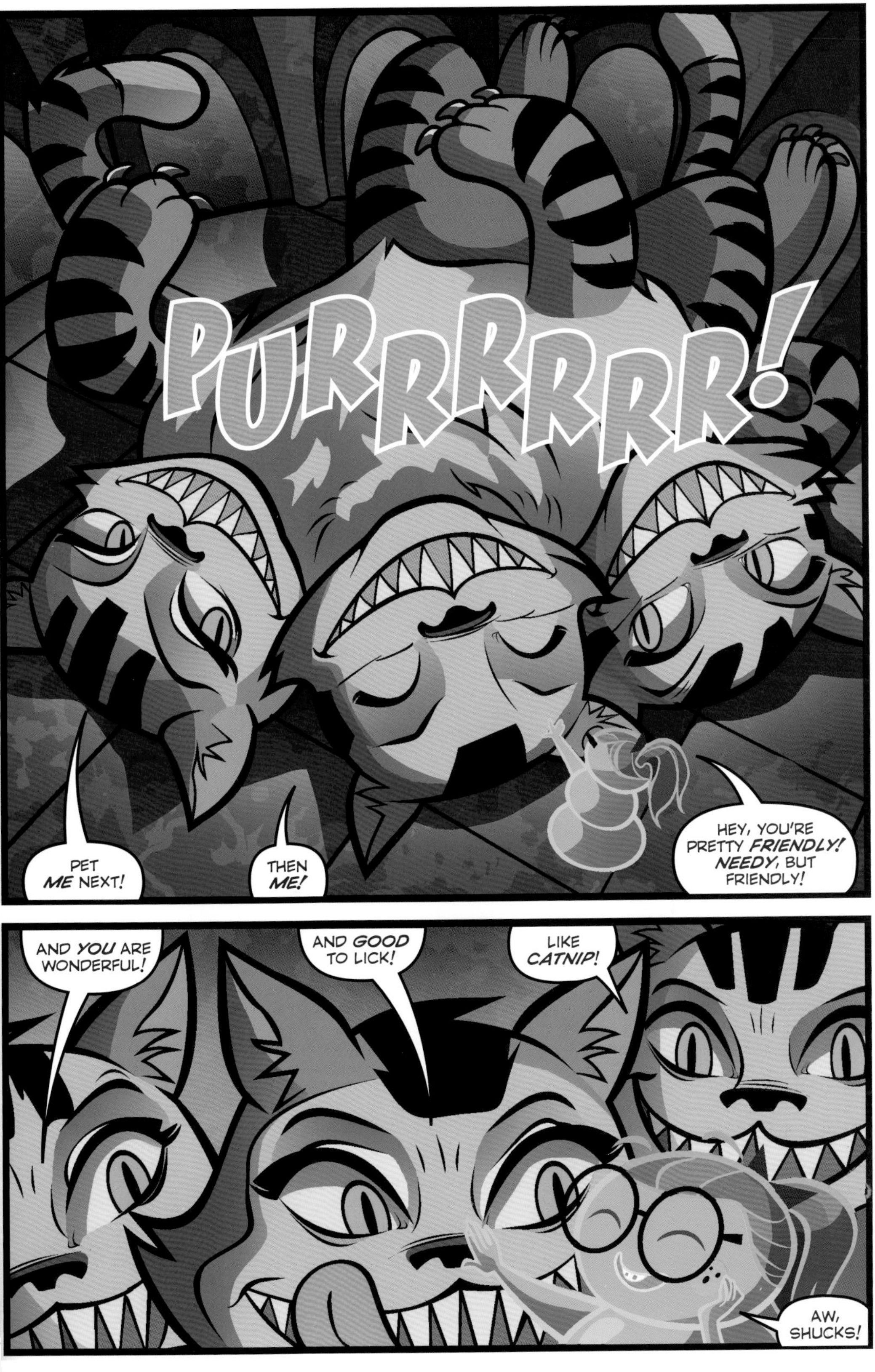
PURRRRRR!
PET ME NEXT!
THEN ME!
HEY, YOU'RE PRETTY FRIENDLY! NEEDY, BUT FRIENDLY!
AND YOU ARE WONDERFUL!
AND GOOD TO LICK!
LIKE CATNIP!
AW, SHUCKS!

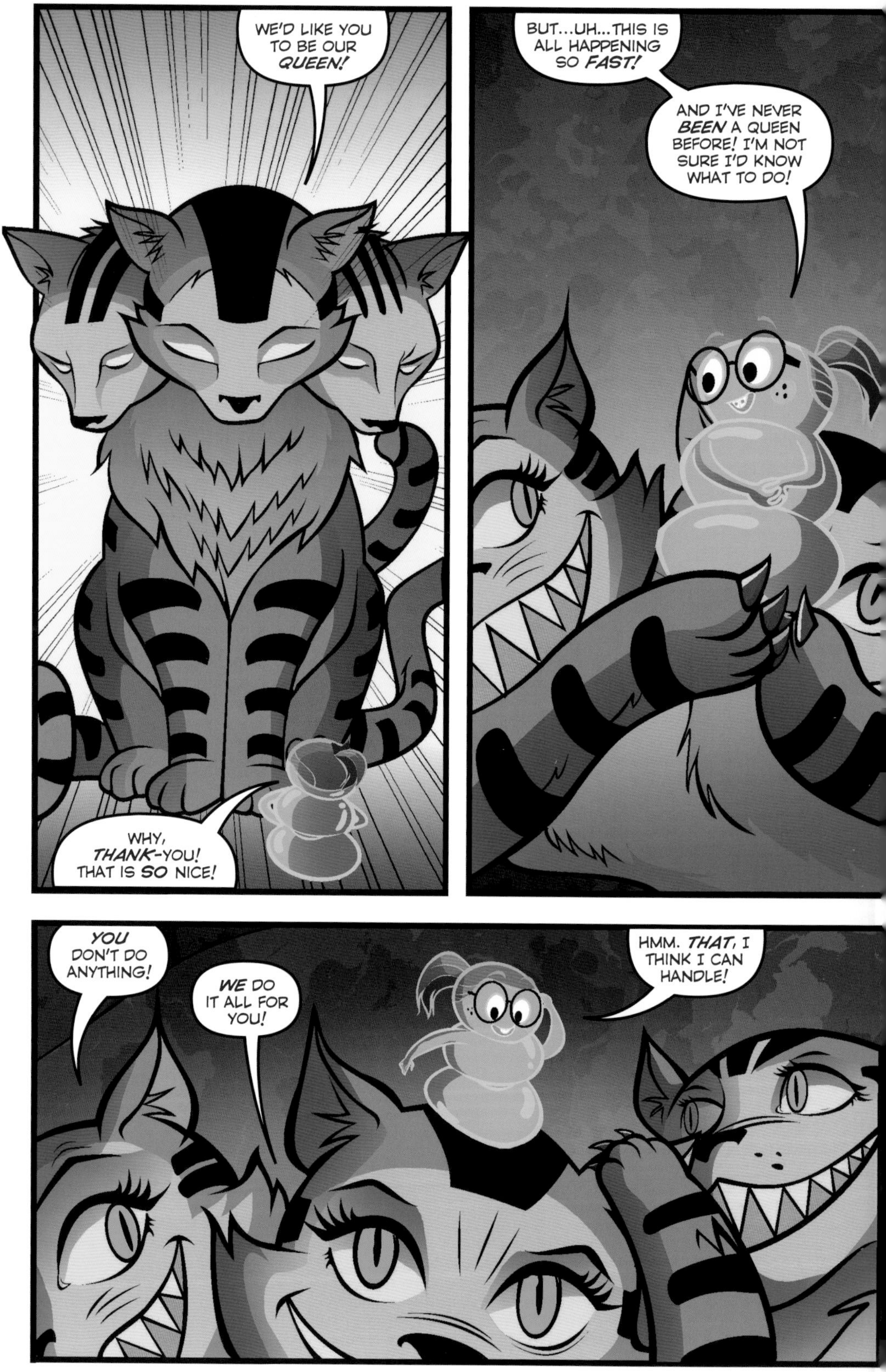
WE'D LIKE YOU TO BE OUR *QUEEN!*
WHY, *THANK*-YOU! THAT IS **SO** NICE!
BUT...UH...THIS IS ALL HAPPENING SO *FAST!*
AND I'VE NEVER *BEEN* A QUEEN BEFORE! I'M NOT SURE I'D KNOW WHAT TO DO!
YOU DON'T DO ANYTHING!
WE DO IT ALL FOR YOU!
HMM. *THAT*, I THINK I CAN HANDLE!

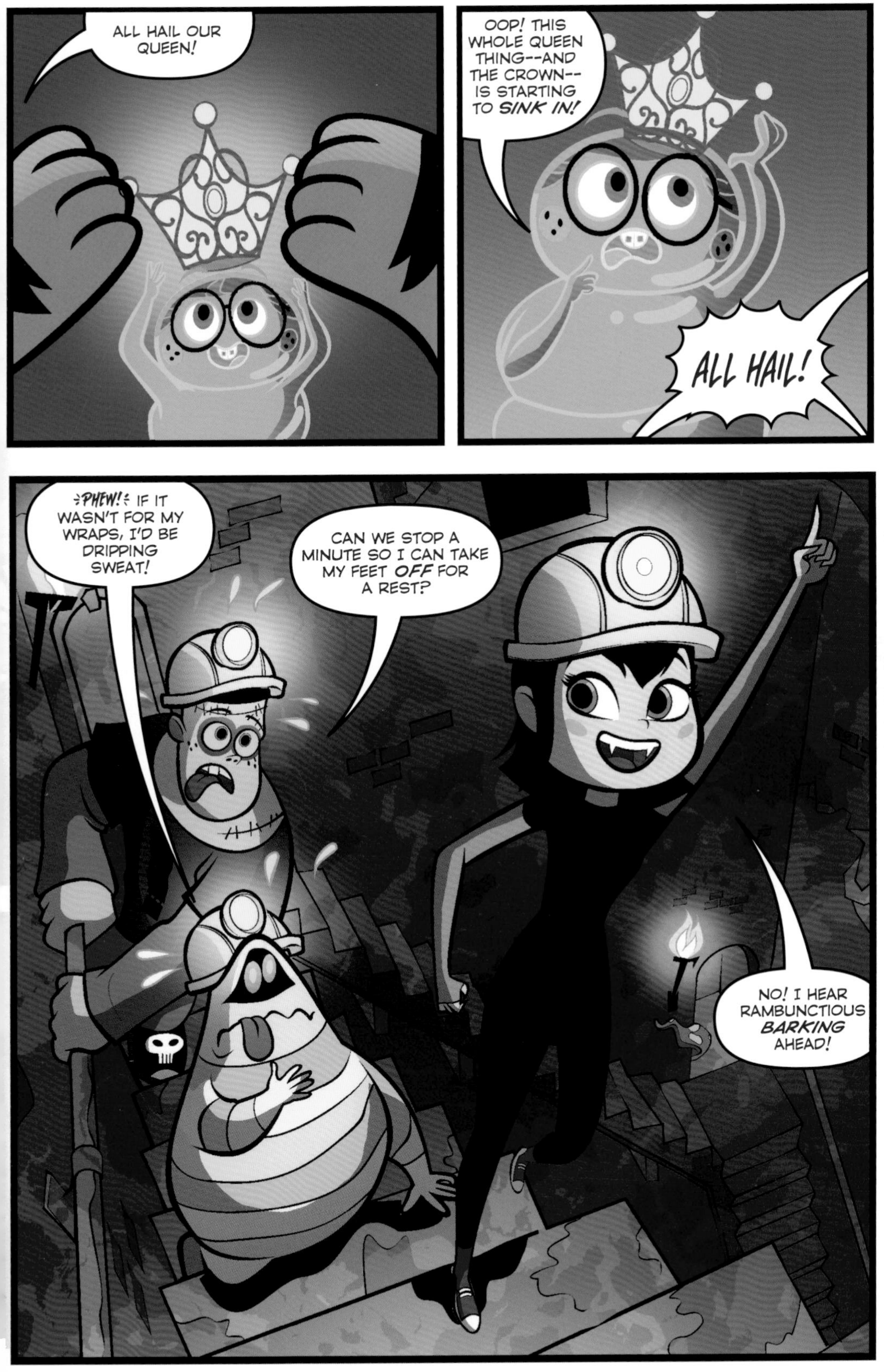
ALL HAIL OUR QUEEN!
OOP! THIS WHOLE QUEEN THING--AND THE CROWN--IS STARTING TO SINK IN!
ALL HAIL!
PHEW! IF IT WASN'T FOR MY WRAPS, I'D BE DRIPPING SWEAT!
CAN WE STOP A MINUTE SO I CAN TAKE MY FEET OFF FOR A REST?
NO! I HEAR RAMBUNCTIOUS BARKING AHEAD!

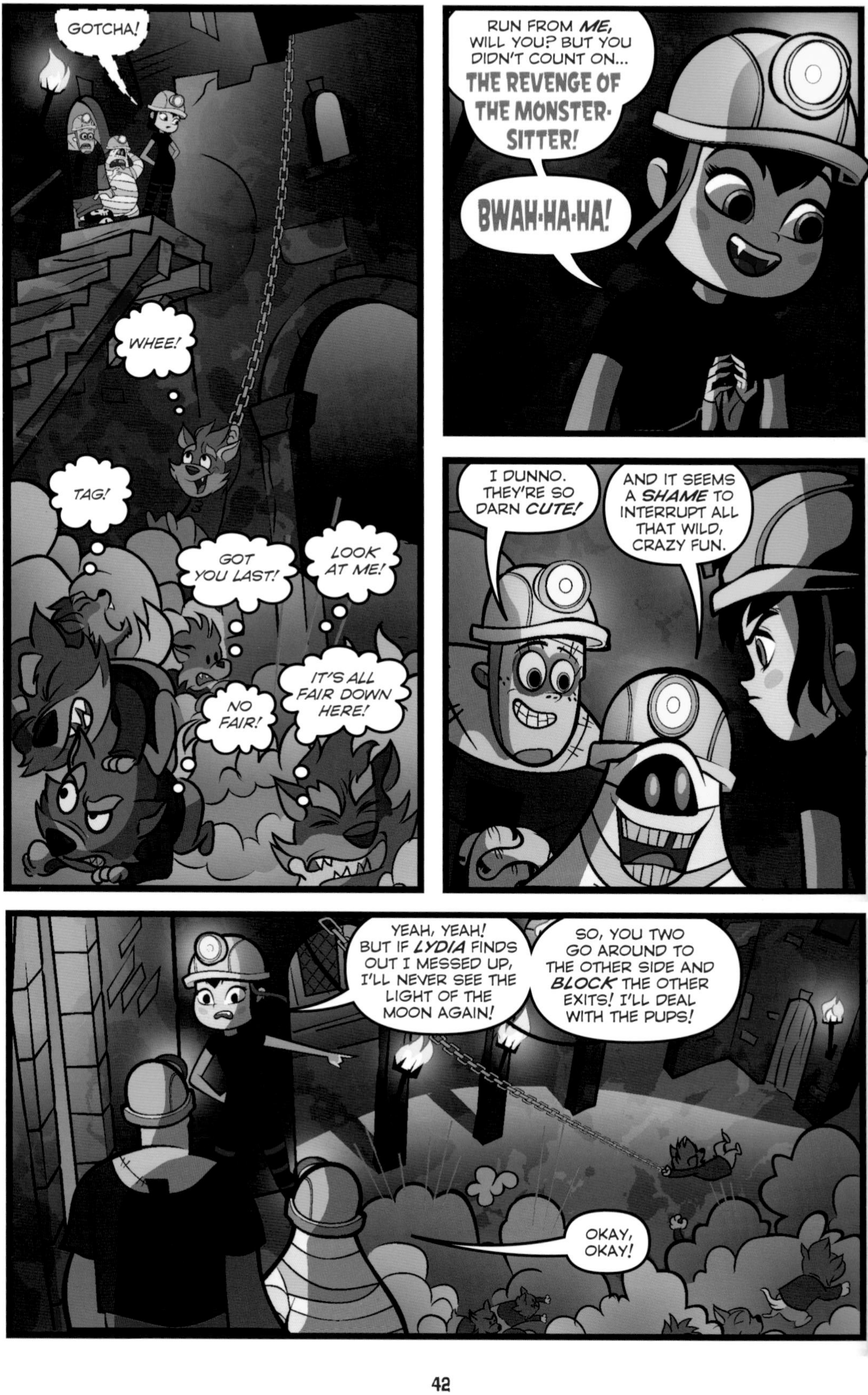
GOTCHA!
WHEE!
TAG!
GOT YOU LAST!
LOOK AT ME!
NO FAIR!
IT'S ALL FAIR DOWN HERE!
RUN FROM ME, WILL YOU? BUT YOU DIDN'T COUNT ON... THE REVENGE OF THE MONSTER-SITTER!
BWAH-HA-HA!
I DUNNO. THEY'RE SO DARN CUTE!
AND IT SEEMS A SHAME TO INTERRUPT ALL THAT WILD, CRAZY FUN.
YEAH, YEAH! BUT IF LYDIA FINDS OUT I MESSED UP, I'LL NEVER SEE THE LIGHT OF THE MOON AGAIN!
SO, YOU TWO GO AROUND TO THE OTHER SIDE AND BLOCK THE OTHER EXITS! I'LL DEAL WITH THE PUPS!
OKAY, OKAY!

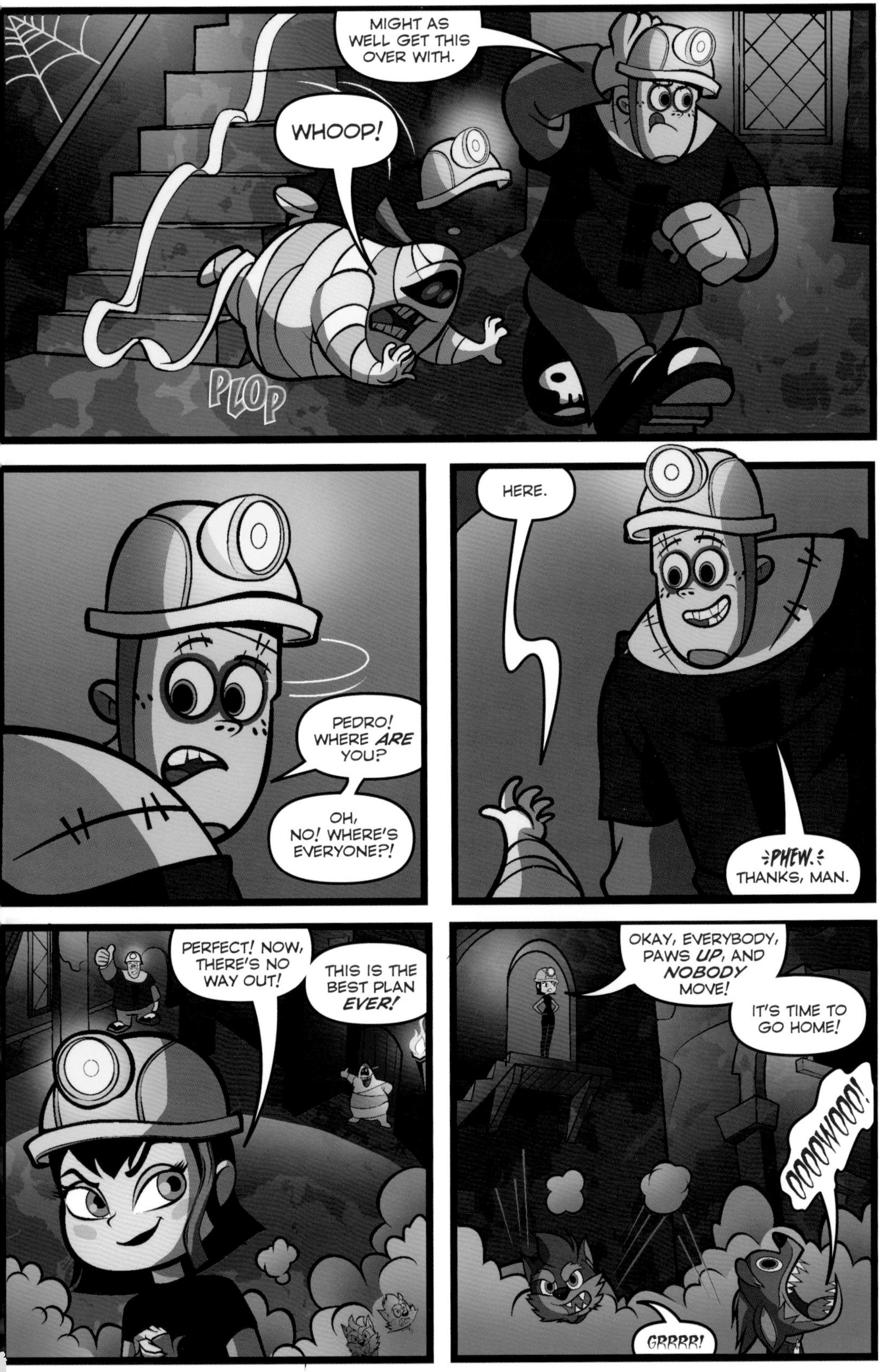
MIGHT AS WELL GET THIS OVER WITH.
WHOOP!
PLOP
PEDRO! WHERE *ARE* YOU?
OH, NO! WHERE'S EVERYONE?!
HERE.
PHEW. THANKS, MAN.
PERFECT! NOW, THERE'S NO WAY OUT!
THIS IS THE BEST PLAN *EVER!*
OKAY, EVERYBODY, PAWS *UP*, AND *NOBODY* MOVE!
IT'S TIME TO GO HOME!
OOOOWOOO!
GRRRR!

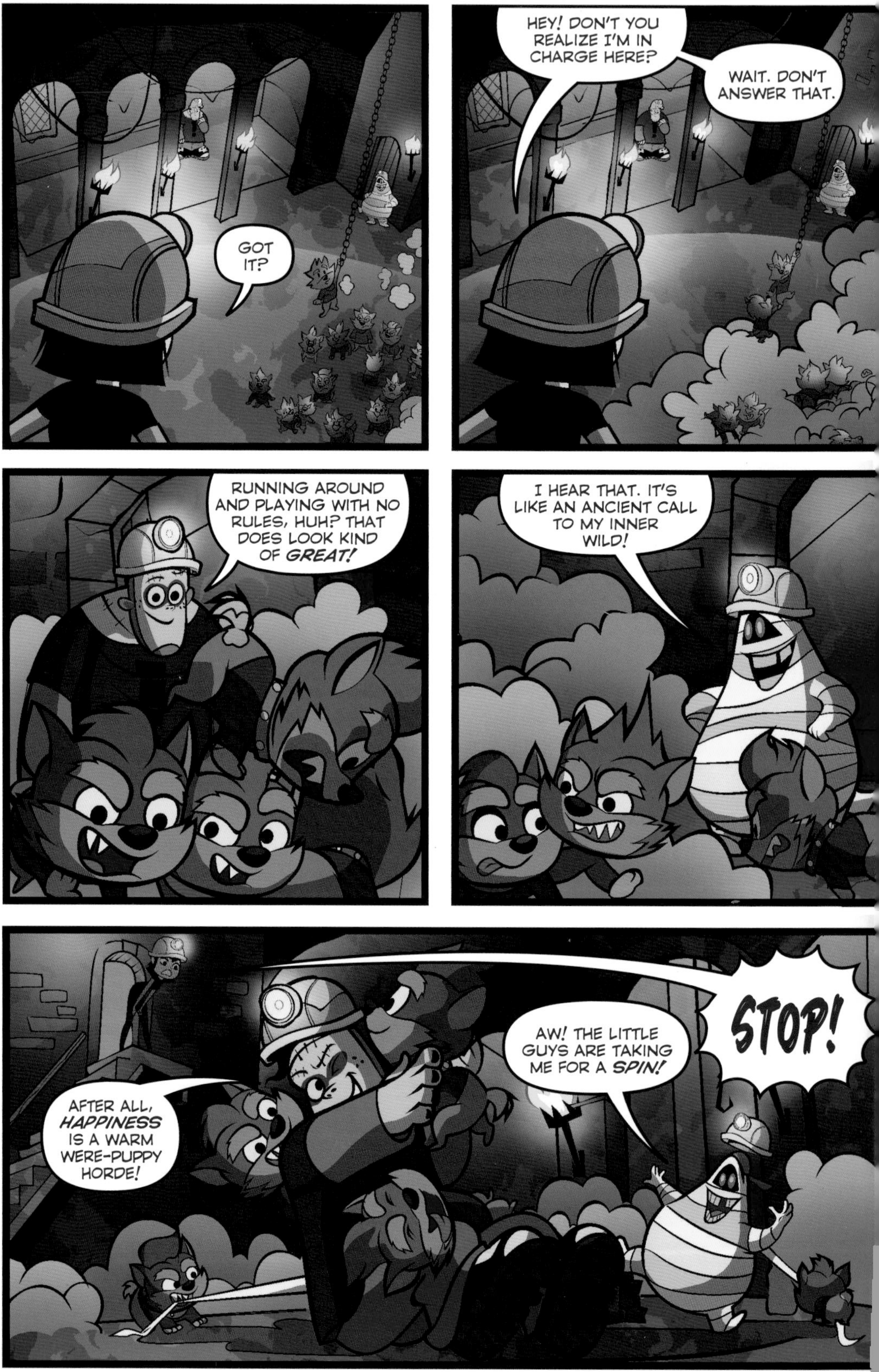
GOT IT?
HEY! DON'T YOU REALIZE I'M IN CHARGE HERE?
WAIT. DON'T ANSWER THAT.
RUNNING AROUND AND PLAYING WITH NO RULES, HUH? THAT DOES LOOK KIND OF *GREAT!*
I HEAR THAT. IT'S LIKE AN ANCIENT CALL TO MY INNER WILD!
STOP!
AW! THE LITTLE GUYS ARE TAKING ME FOR A *SPIN!*
AFTER ALL, *HAPPINESS* IS A WARM WERE-PUPPY HORDE!

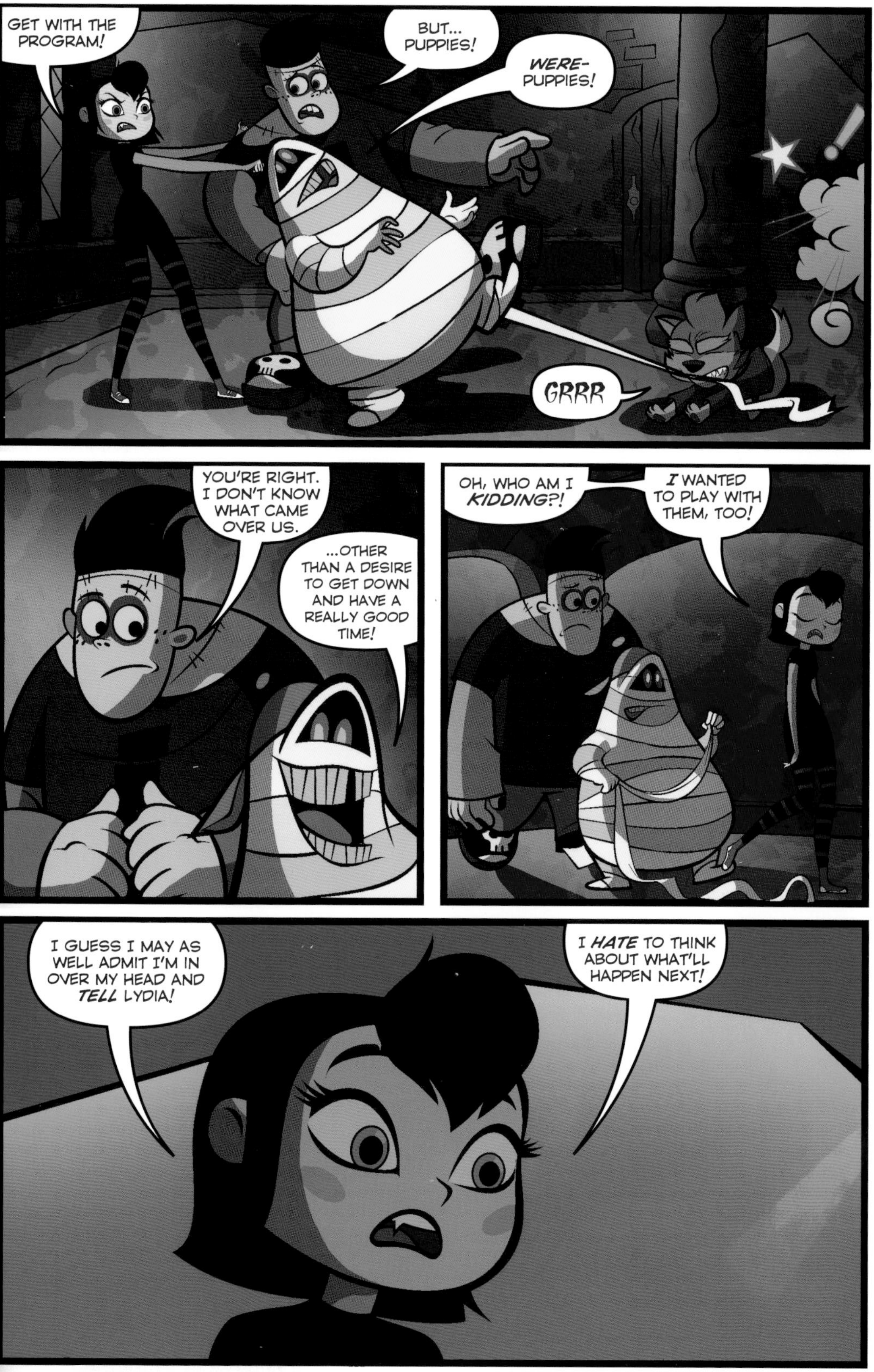
GET WITH THE PROGRAM!
BUT... PUPPIES!
*WERE-*PUPPIES!
GRRR
YOU'RE RIGHT. I DON'T KNOW WHAT CAME OVER US.
...OTHER THAN A DESIRE TO GET DOWN AND HAVE A REALLY GOOD TIME!
OH, WHO AM I *KIDDING*?!
I WANTED TO PLAY WITH THEM, TOO!
I GUESS I MAY AS WELL ADMIT I'M IN OVER MY HEAD AND *TELL* LYDIA!
I *HATE* TO THINK ABOUT WHAT'LL HAPPEN NEXT!

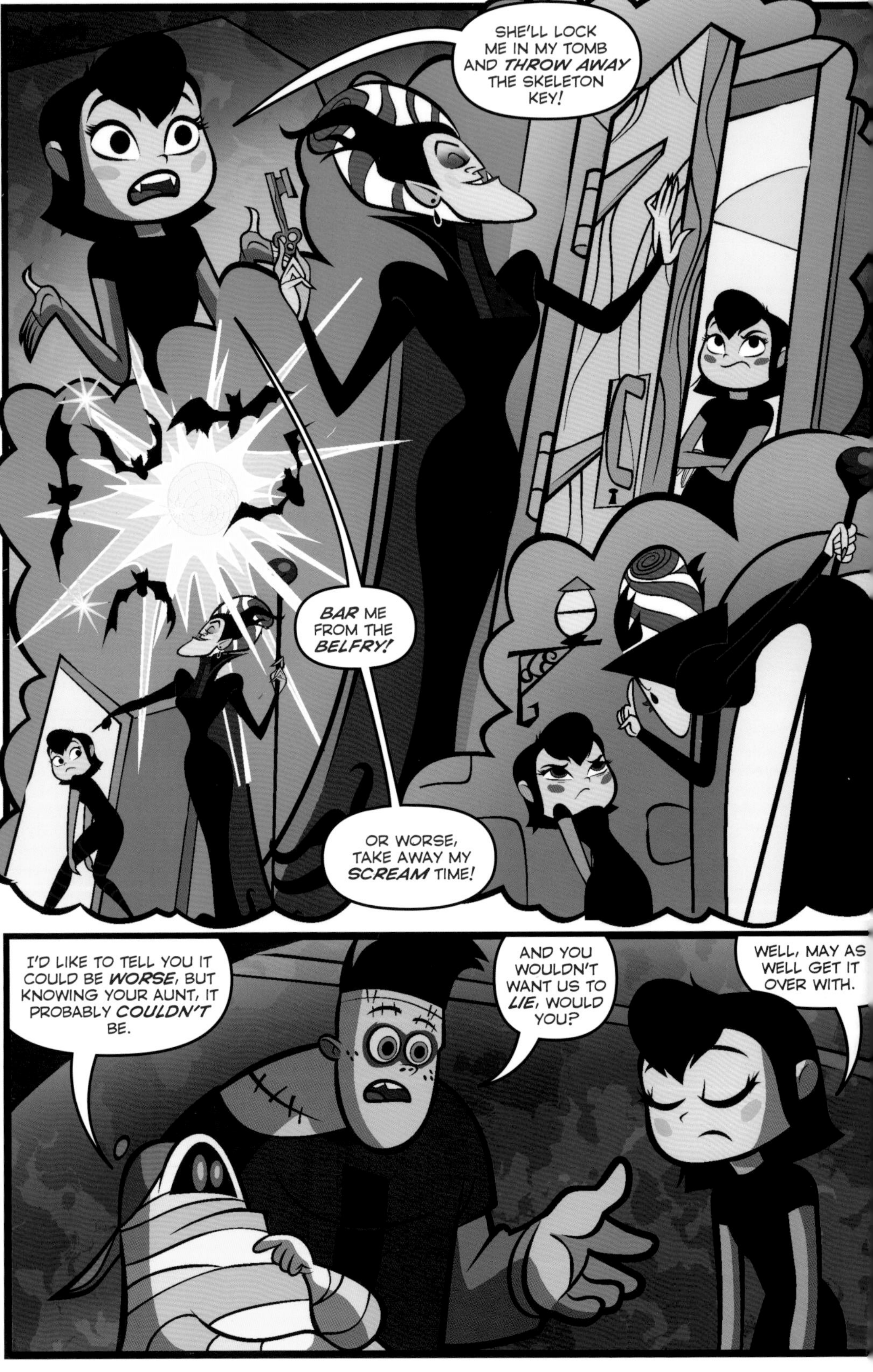
SHE'LL LOCK ME IN MY TOMB AND THROW AWAY THE SKELETON KEY!
BAR ME FROM THE BELFRY!
OR WORSE, TAKE AWAY MY SCREAM TIME!
I'D LIKE TO TELL YOU IT COULD BE WORSE, BUT KNOWING YOUR AUNT, IT PROBABLY COULDN'T BE.
AND YOU WOULDN'T WANT US TO LIE, WOULD YOU?
WELL, MAY AS WELL GET IT OVER WITH.

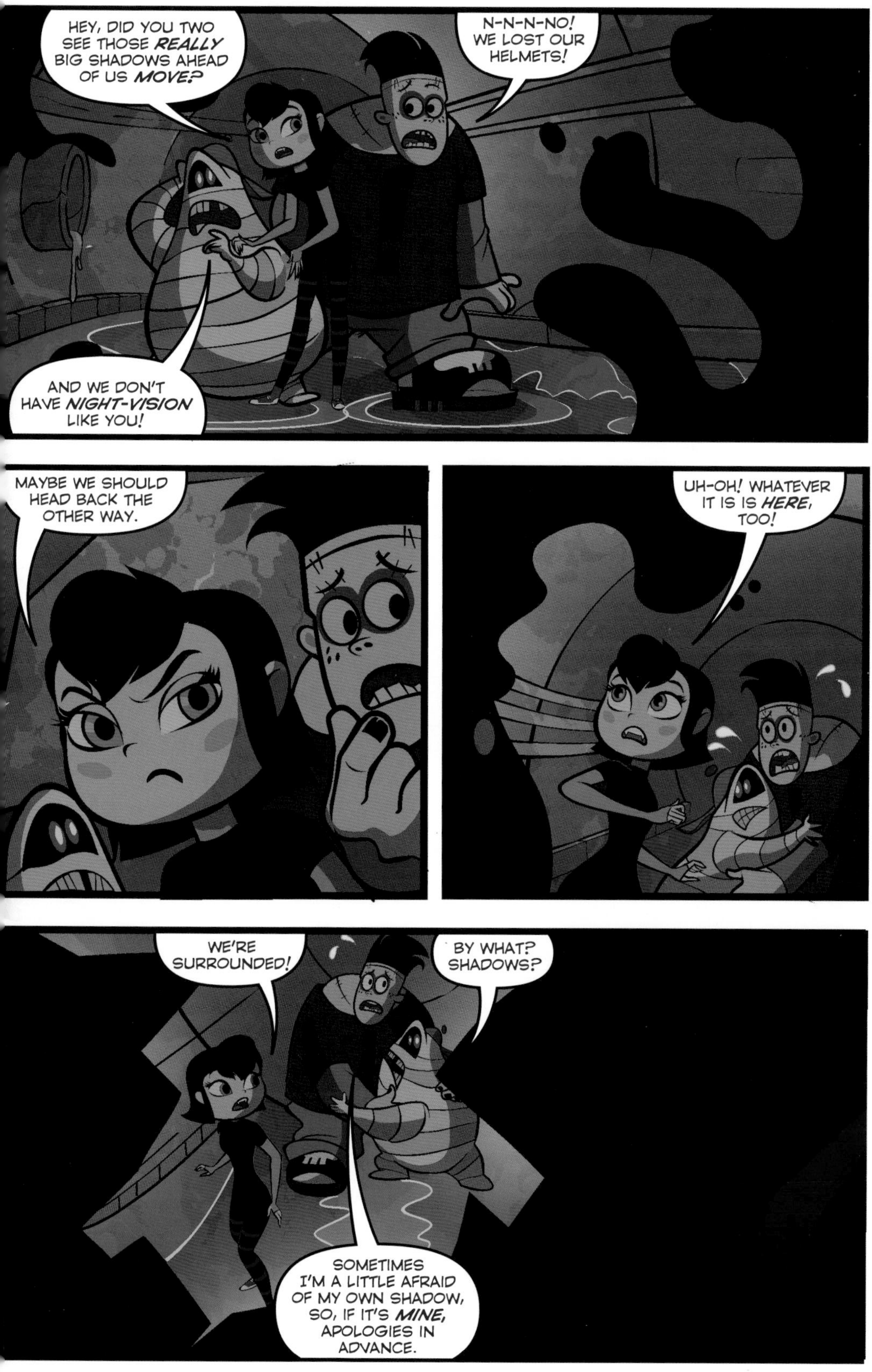

HEY, DID YOU TWO SEE THOSE REALLY BIG SHADOWS AHEAD OF US MOVE?
N-N-N-NO! WE LOST OUR HELMETS!
AND WE DON'T HAVE NIGHT-VISION LIKE YOU!
MAYBE WE SHOULD HEAD BACK THE OTHER WAY.
UH-OH! WHATEVER IT IS IS HERE, TOO!
WE'RE SURROUNDED!
BY WHAT? SHADOWS?
SOMETIMES I'M A LITTLE AFRAID OF MY OWN SHADOW, SO, IF IT'S MINE, APOLOGIES IN ADVANCE.

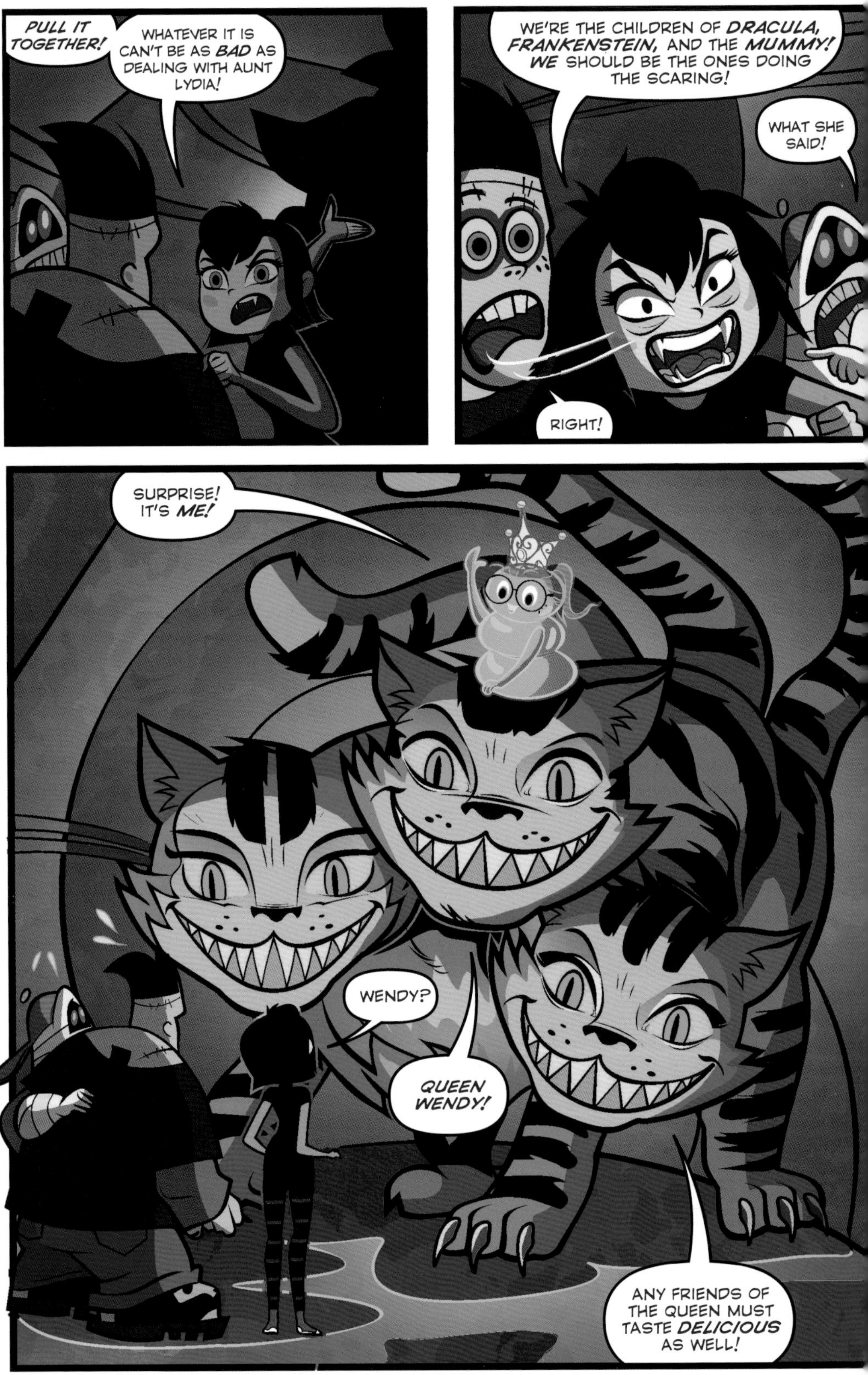
PULL IT TOGETHER!
WHATEVER IT IS CAN'T BE AS BAD AS DEALING WITH AUNT LYDIA!
WE'RE THE CHILDREN OF DRACULA, FRANKENSTEIN, AND THE MUMMY! WE SHOULD BE THE ONES DOING THE SCARING!
WHAT SHE SAID!
RIGHT!
SURPRISE! IT'S ME!
WENDY?
QUEEN WENDY!
ANY FRIENDS OF THE QUEEN MUST TASTE DELICIOUS AS WELL!

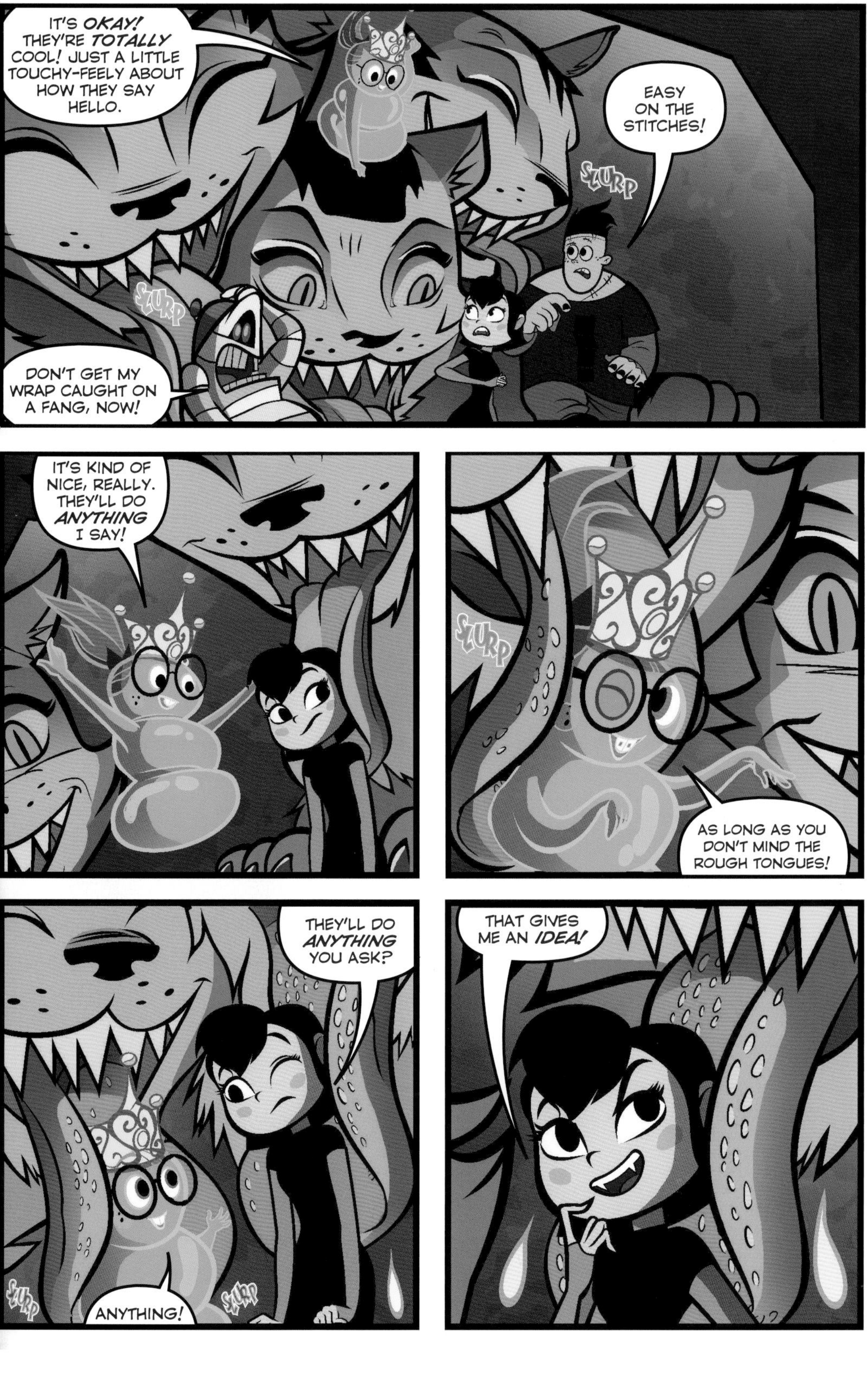
IT'S *OKAY!* THEY'RE *TOTALLY* COOL! JUST A LITTLE TOUCHY-FEELY ABOUT HOW THEY SAY HELLO.
EASY ON THE STITCHES!
SLURP
SLURP
DON'T GET MY WRAP CAUGHT ON A FANG, NOW!
IT'S KIND OF NICE, REALLY. THEY'LL DO *ANYTHING* I SAY!
SLURP
AS LONG AS YOU DON'T MIND THE ROUGH TONGUES!
THEY'LL DO *ANYTHING* YOU ASK?
SLURP
ANYTHING!
SLURP
THAT GIVES ME AN *IDEA!*

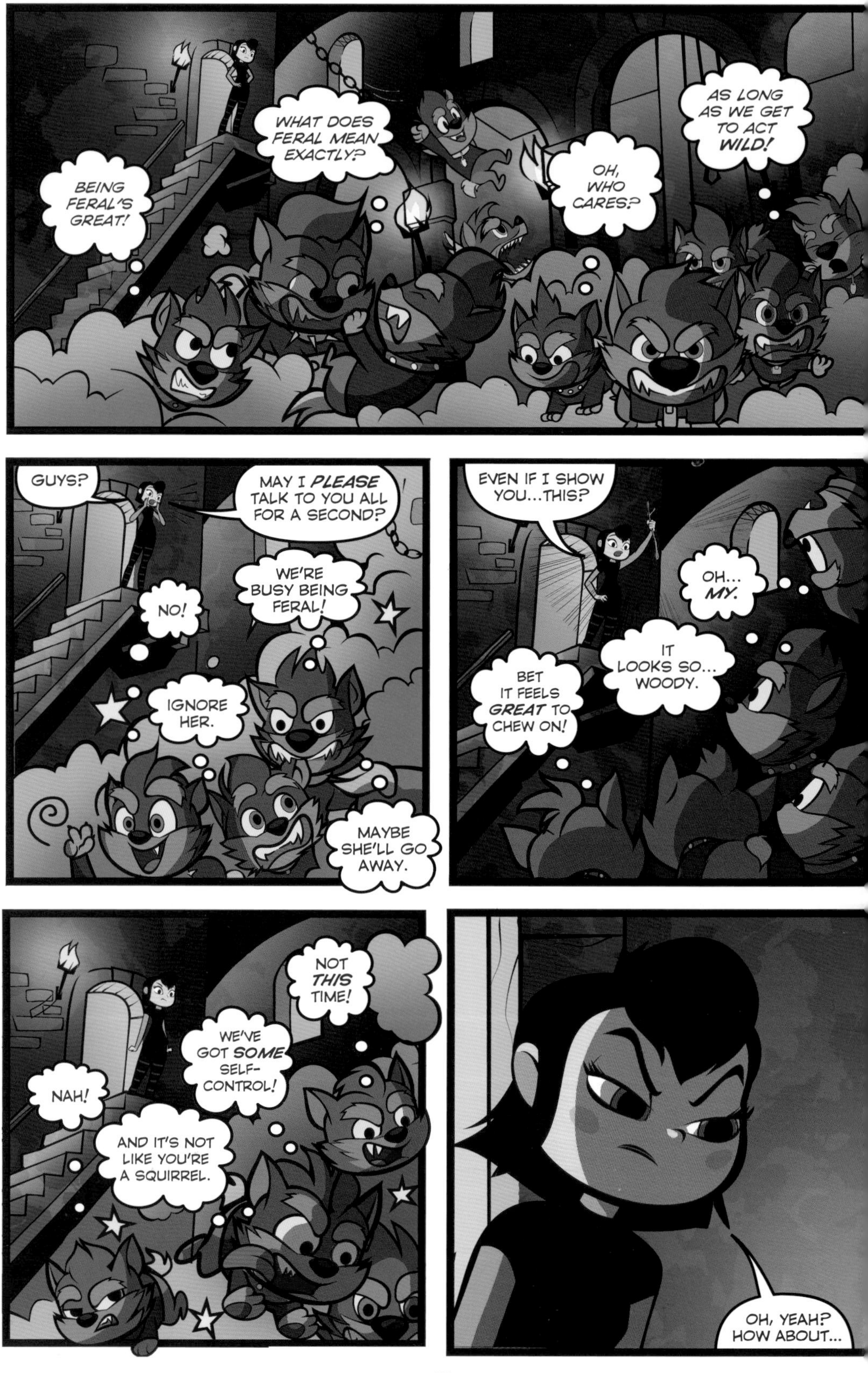
BEING FERAL'S GREAT!
WHAT DOES FERAL MEAN EXACTLY?
OH, WHO CARES?
AS LONG AS WE GET TO ACT WILD!
GUYS?
MAY I PLEASE TALK TO YOU ALL FOR A SECOND?
NO!
WE'RE BUSY BEING FERAL!
IGNORE HER.
MAYBE SHE'LL GO AWAY.
EVEN IF I SHOW YOU...THIS?
OH... MY.
IT LOOKS SO... WOODY.
BET IT FEELS GREAT TO CHEW ON!
NOT THIS TIME!
WE'VE GOT SOME SELF-CONTROL!
NAH!
AND IT'S NOT LIKE YOU'RE A SQUIRREL.
OH, YEAH? HOW ABOUT...

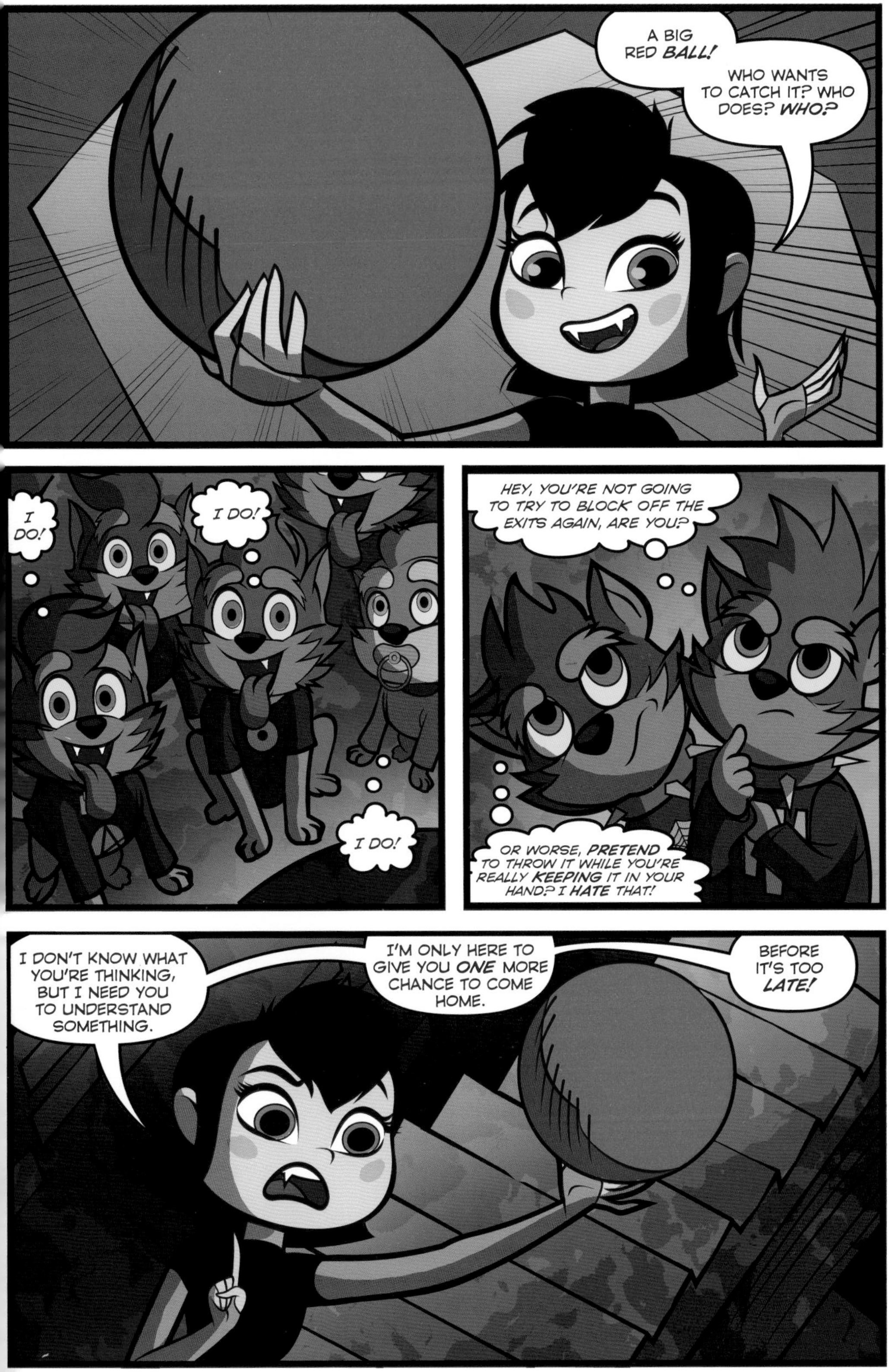
A BIG RED *BALL!*
WHO WANTS TO CATCH IT? WHO DOES? *WHO?*
I DO!
I DO!
I DO!
HEY, YOU'RE NOT GOING TO TRY TO BLOCK OFF THE EXITS AGAIN, ARE YOU?
OR WORSE, **PRETEND** TO THROW IT WHILE YOU'RE REALLY **KEEPING** IT IN YOUR HAND? I **HATE** THAT!
I DON'T KNOW WHAT YOU'RE THINKING, BUT I NEED YOU TO UNDERSTAND SOMETHING.
I'M ONLY HERE TO GIVE YOU *ONE* MORE CHANCE TO COME HOME.
BEFORE IT'S TOO *LATE!*

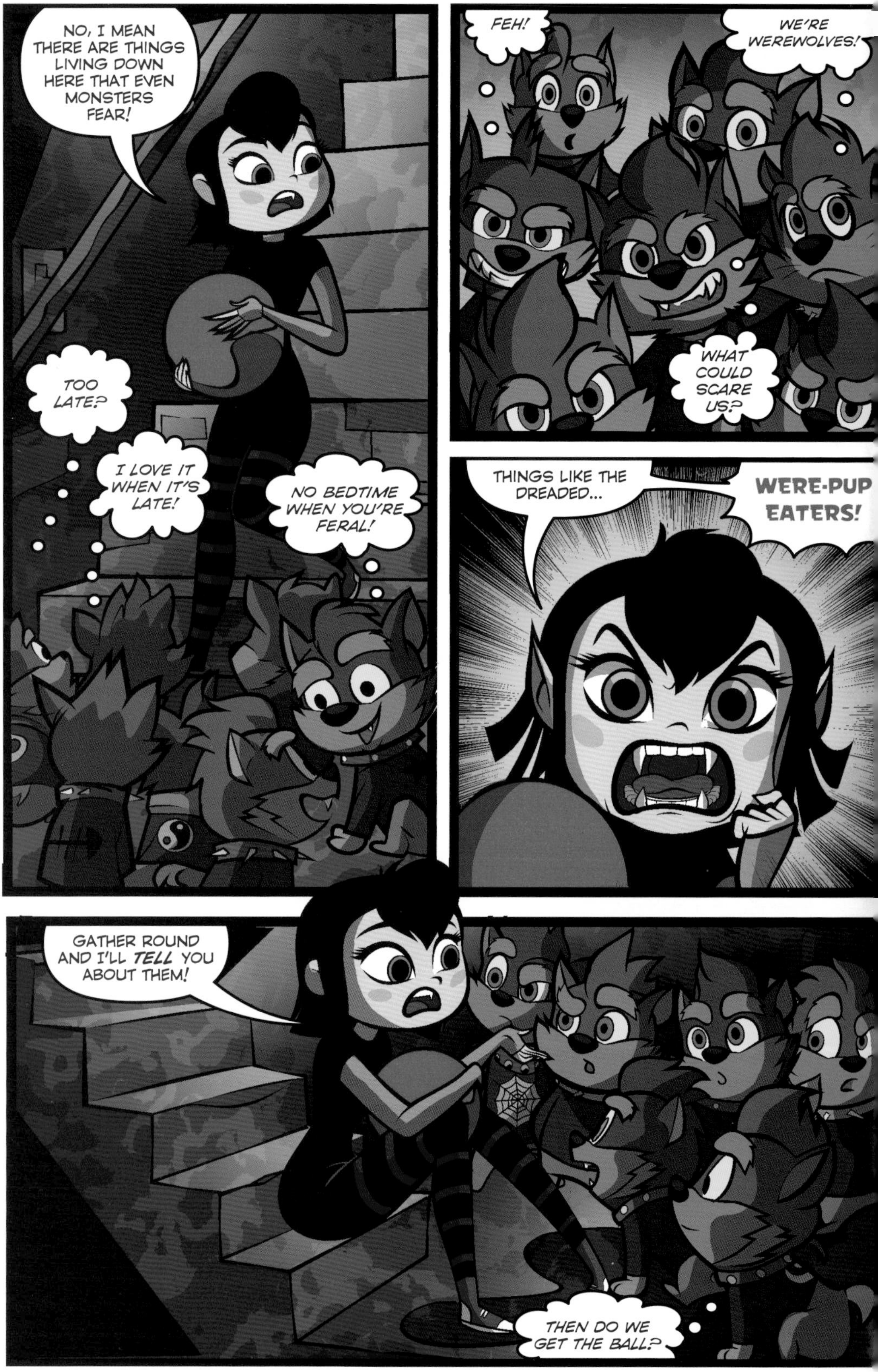
NO, I MEAN THERE ARE THINGS LIVING DOWN HERE THAT EVEN MONSTERS FEAR!
TOO LATE?
I LOVE IT WHEN IT'S LATE!
NO BEDTIME WHEN YOU'RE FERAL!
FEH!
WE'RE WEREWOLVES!
WHAT COULD SCARE US?
THINGS LIKE THE DREADED...
WERE-PUP EATERS!
GATHER ROUND AND I'LL TELL YOU ABOUT THEM!
THEN DO WE GET THE BALL?

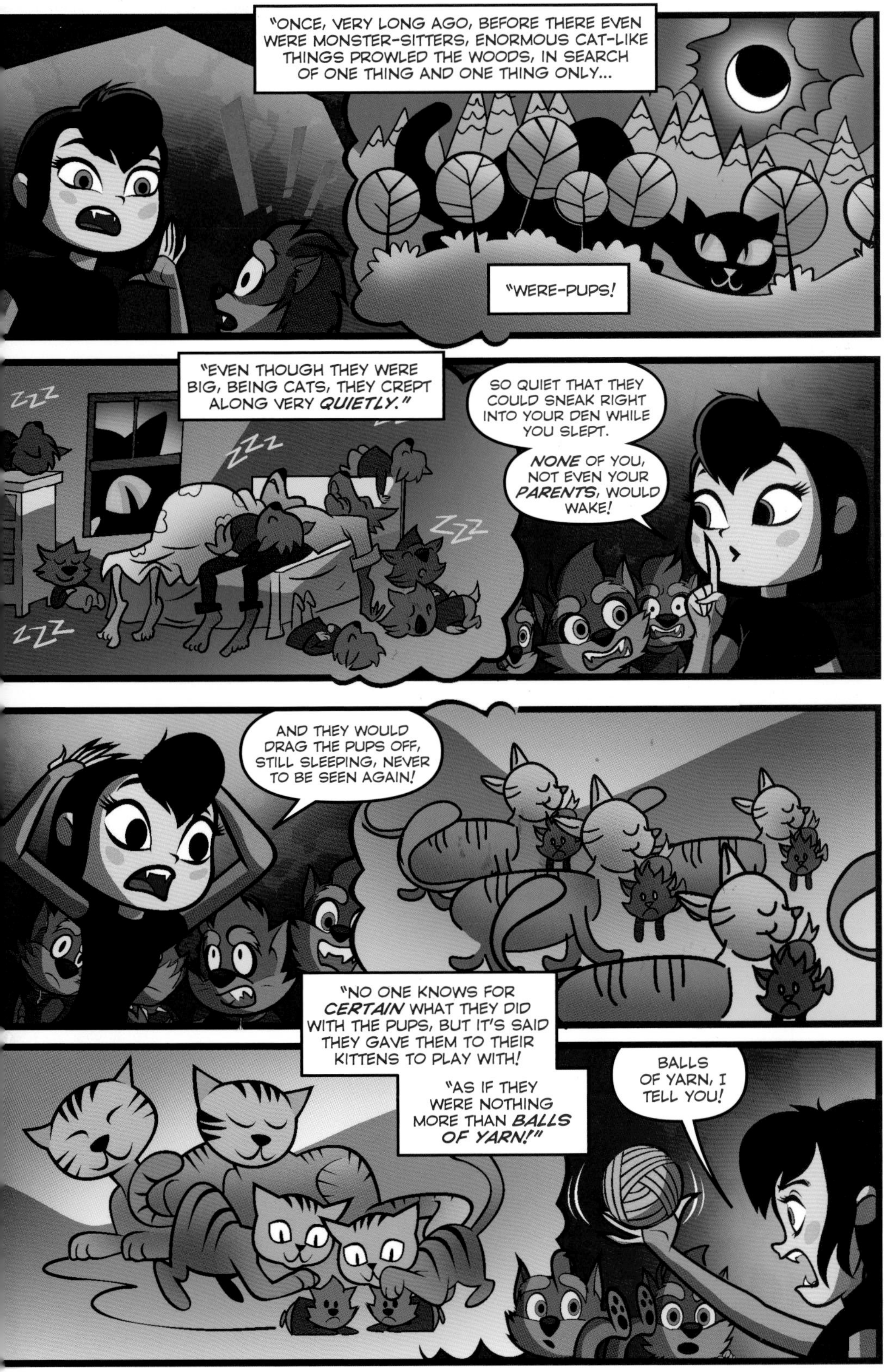
"ONCE, VERY LONG AGO, BEFORE THERE EVEN WERE MONSTER-SITTERS, ENORMOUS CAT-LIKE THINGS PROWLED THE WOODS, IN SEARCH OF ONE THING AND ONE THING ONLY...
"WERE-PUPS!
"EVEN THOUGH THEY WERE BIG, BEING CATS, THEY CREPT ALONG VERY *QUIETLY.*"
SO QUIET THAT THEY COULD SNEAK RIGHT INTO YOUR DEN WHILE YOU SLEPT.
NONE OF YOU, NOT EVEN YOUR *PARENTS*, WOULD WAKE!
ZZZ
ZZZ
ZZZ
ZZZ
AND THEY WOULD DRAG THE PUPS OFF, STILL SLEEPING, NEVER TO BE SEEN AGAIN!
"NO ONE KNOWS FOR *CERTAIN* WHAT THEY DID WITH THE PUPS, BUT IT'S SAID THEY GAVE THEM TO THEIR KITTENS TO PLAY WITH!
"AS IF THEY WERE NOTHING MORE THAN *BALLS OF YARN!*"
BALLS OF YARN, I TELL YOU!

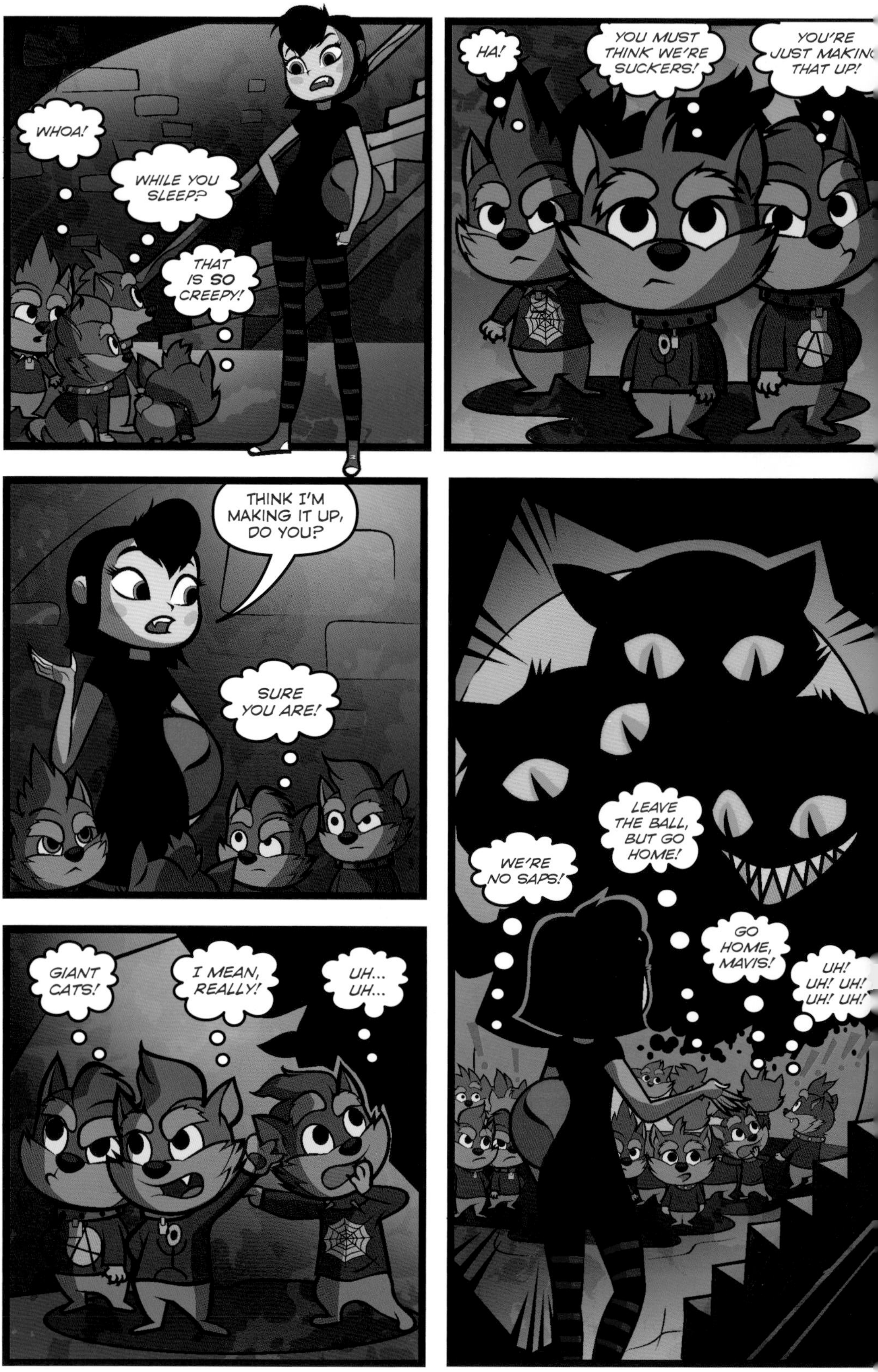
WHOA!
WHILE YOU SLEEP?
THAT IS SO CREEPY!
HA!
YOU MUST THINK WE'RE SUCKERS!
YOU'RE JUST MAKIN THAT UP!
THINK I'M MAKING IT UP, DO YOU?
SURE YOU ARE!
GIANT CATS!
I MEAN, REALLY!
UH... UH...
WE'RE NO SAPS!
LEAVE THE BALL, BUT GO HOME!
GO HOME, MAVIS!
UH! UH! UH! UH! UH!

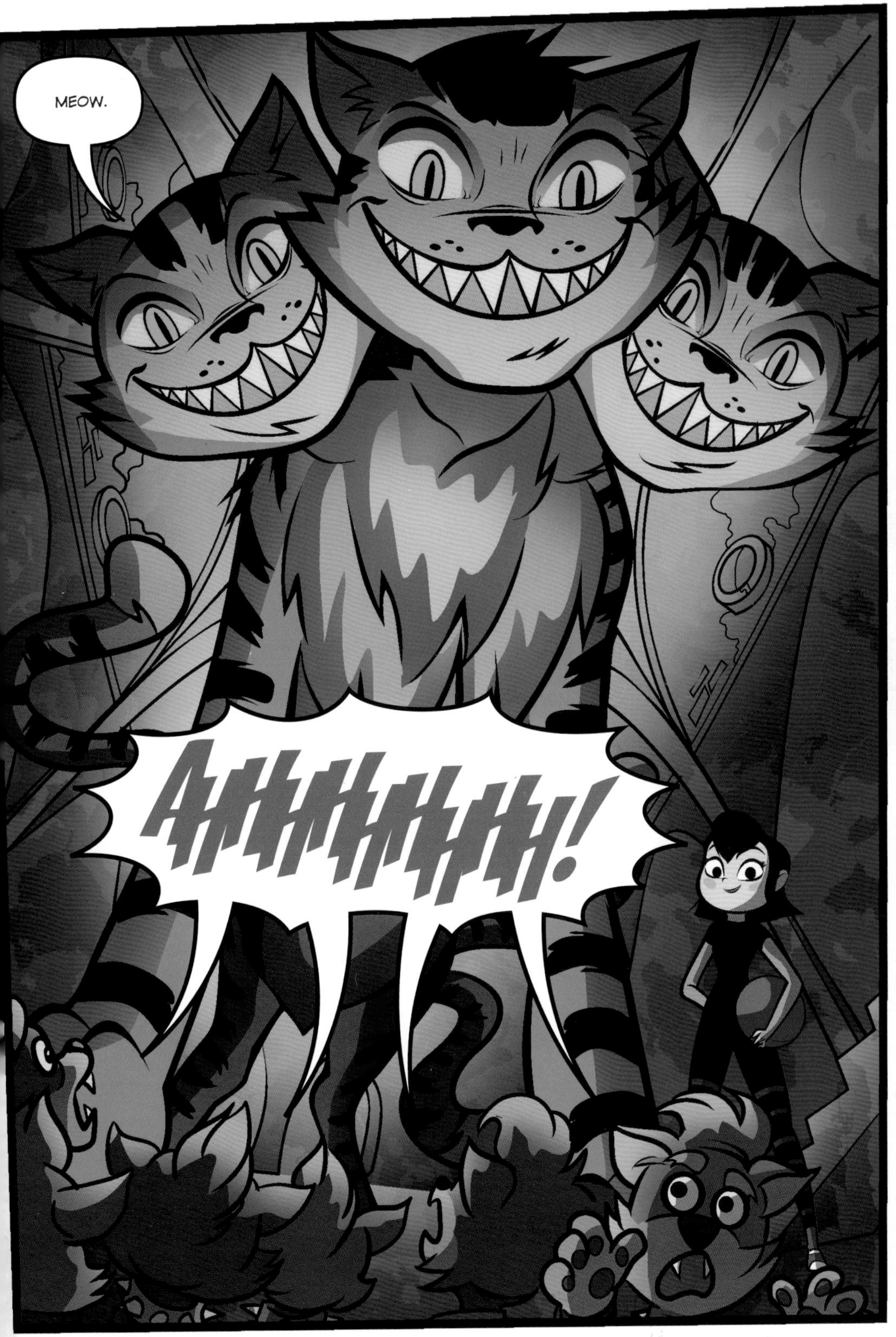
MEOW.
AHHHHHHHHH!

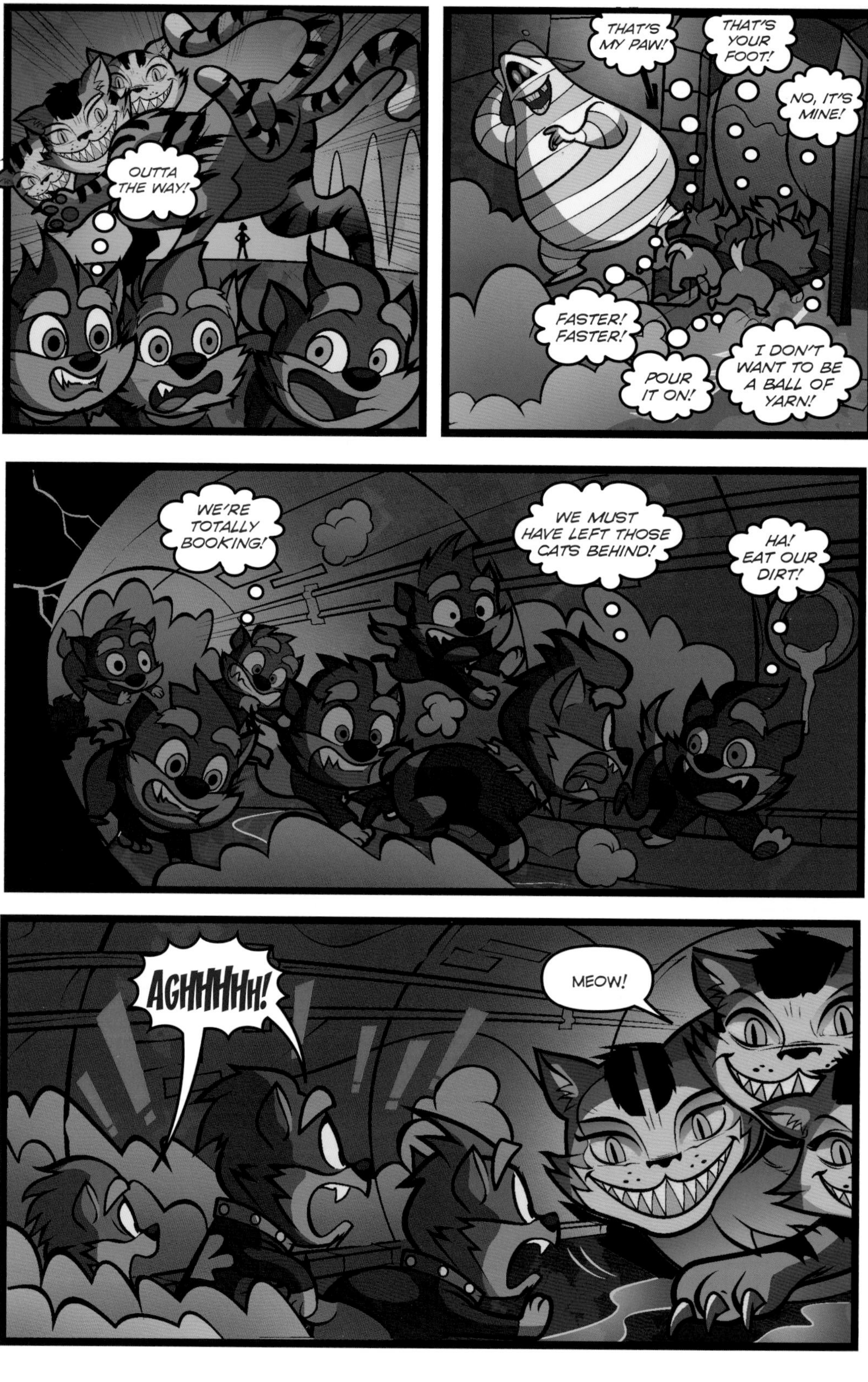
OUTTA THE WAY!
THAT'S MY PAW!
THAT'S YOUR FOOT!
NO, IT'S MINE!
FASTER! FASTER!
POUR IT ON!
I DON'T WANT TO BE A BALL OF YARN!
WE'RE TOTALLY BOOKING!
WE MUST HAVE LEFT THOSE CATS BEHIND!
HA! EAT OUR DIRT!
AGHHHHH!
MEOW!

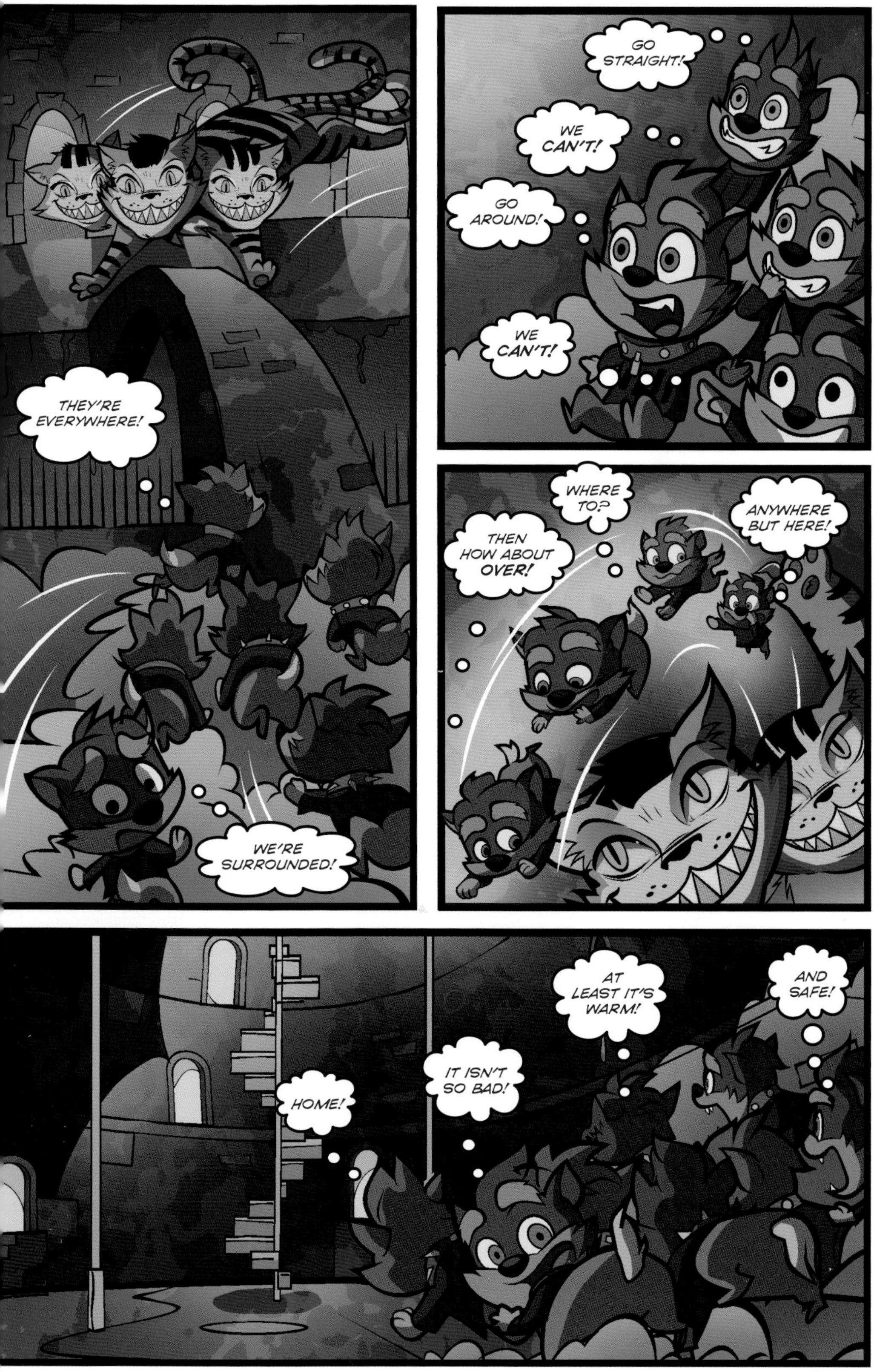
THEY'RE EVERYWHERE!
WE'RE SURROUNDED!
GO STRAIGHT!
WE CAN'T!
GO AROUND!
WE CAN'T!
THEN HOW ABOUT OVER!
WHERE TO?
ANYWHERE BUT HERE!
HOME!
IT ISN'T SO BAD!
AT LEAST IT'S WARM!
AND SAFE!

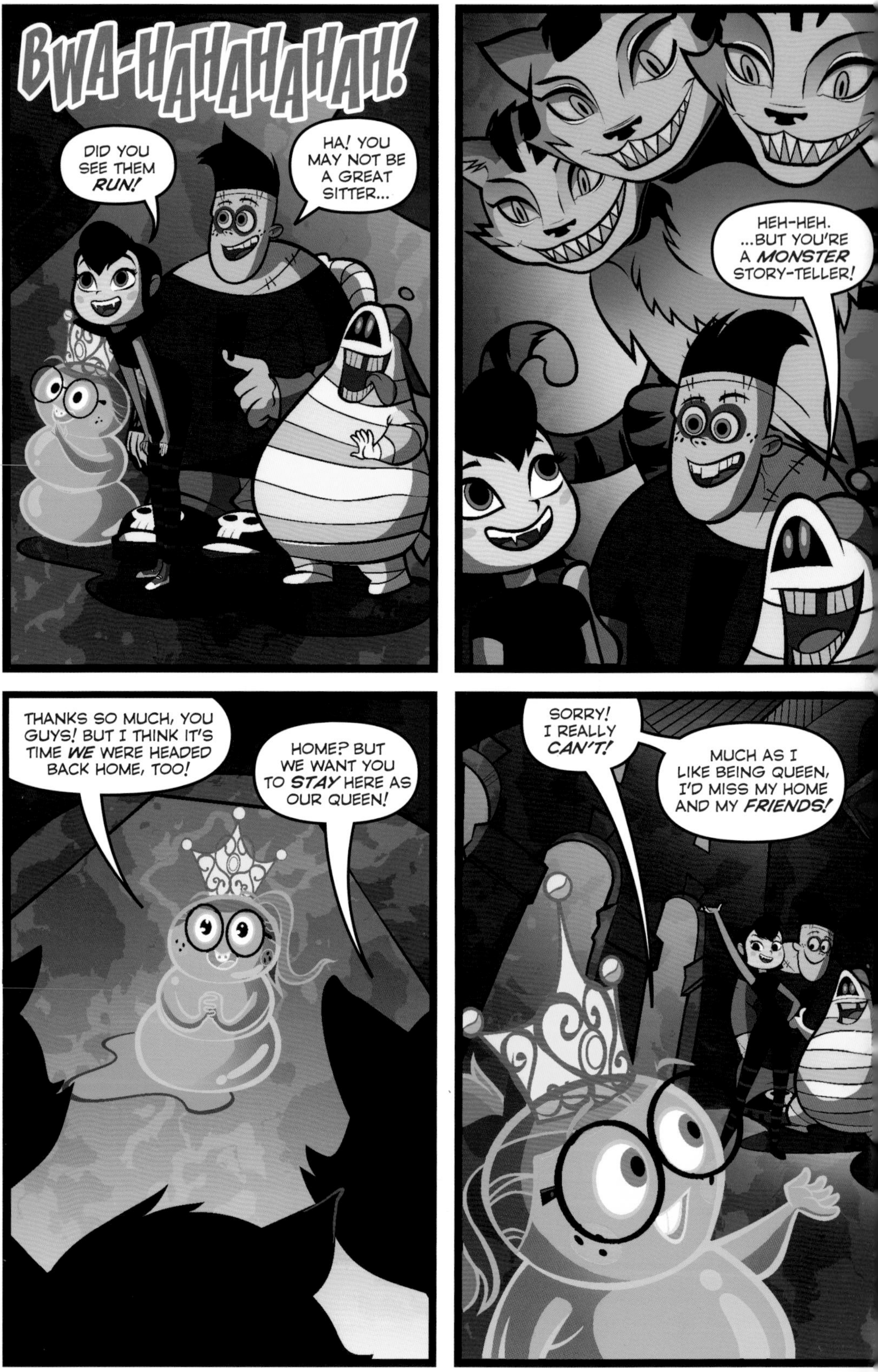
BWA-HAHAHAHAHAH!
DID YOU SEE THEM *RUN!*
HA! YOU MAY NOT BE A GREAT SITTER...
HEH-HEH. ...BUT YOU'RE A *MONSTER* STORY-TELLER!
THANKS SO MUCH, YOU GUYS! BUT I THINK IT'S TIME *WE* WERE HEADED BACK HOME, TOO!
HOME? BUT WE WANT YOU TO *STAY* HERE AS OUR QUEEN!
SORRY! I REALLY *CAN'T!*
MUCH AS I LIKE BEING QUEEN, I'D MISS MY HOME AND MY *FRIENDS!*

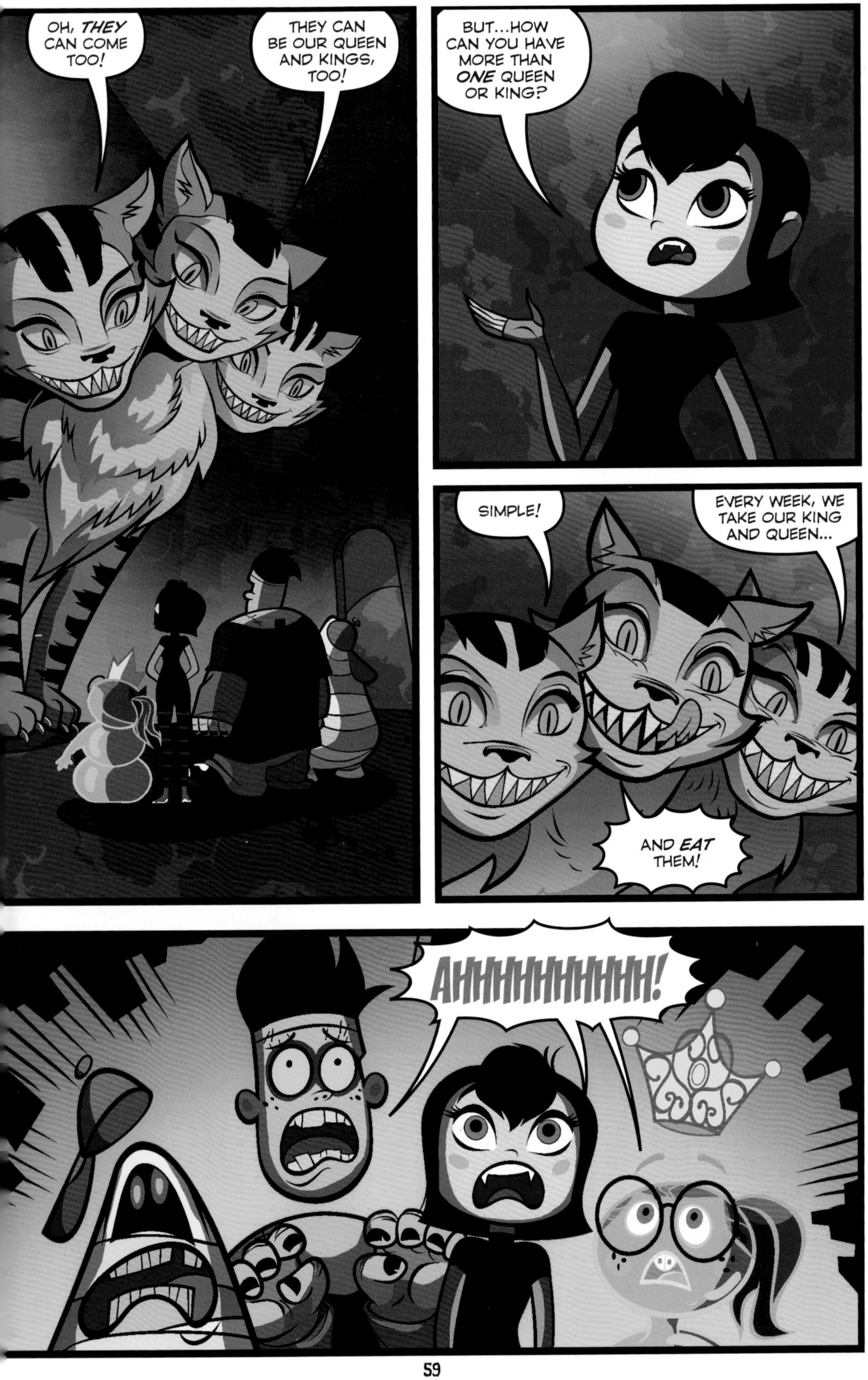
OH, THEY CAN COME TOO!
THEY CAN BE OUR QUEEN AND KINGS, TOO!
BUT...HOW CAN YOU HAVE MORE THAN ONE QUEEN OR KING?
SIMPLE!
EVERY WEEK, WE TAKE OUR KING AND QUEEN...
AND EAT THEM!
AHHHHHHHHHH!

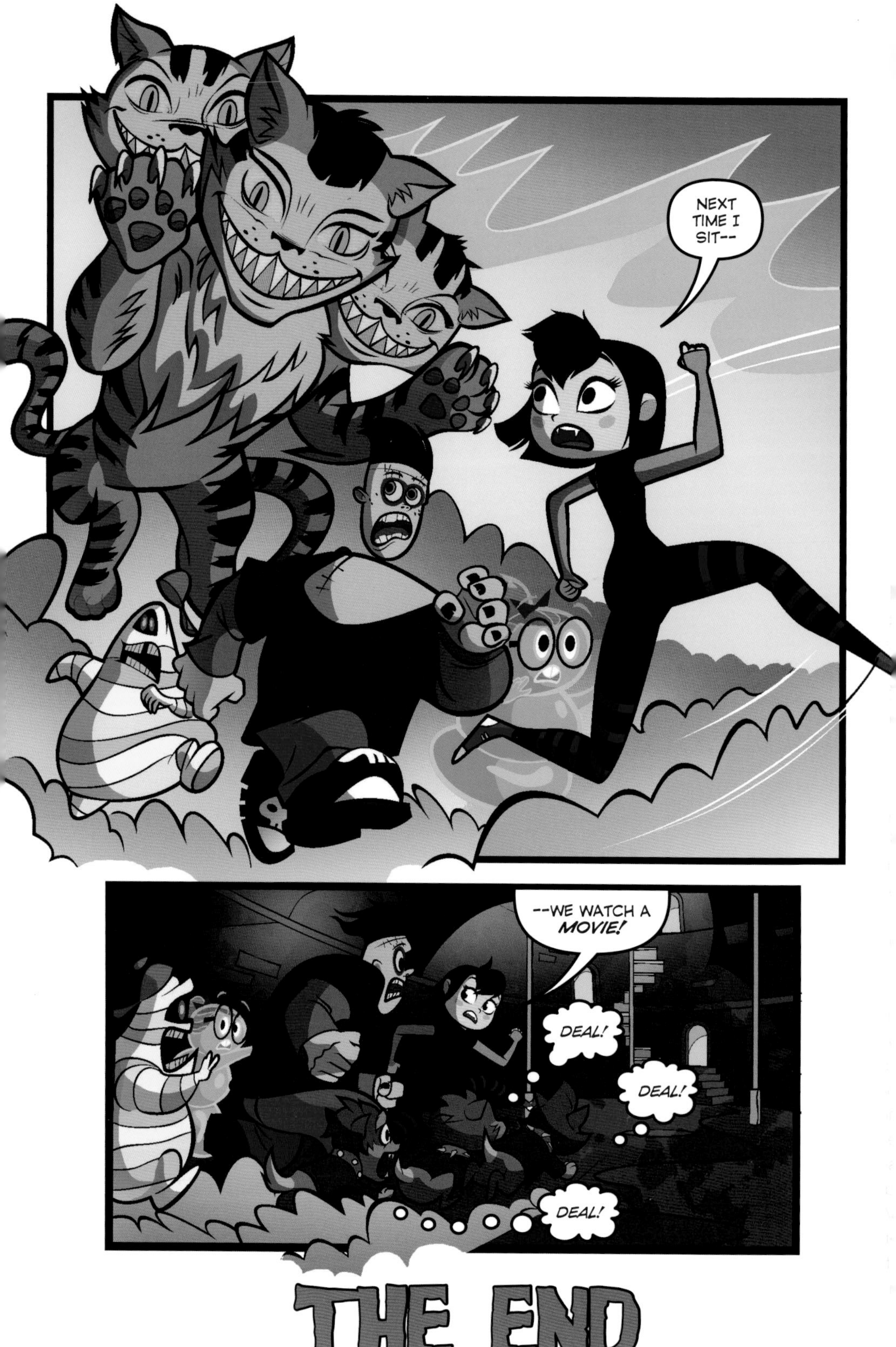
NEXT TIME I SIT--
--WE WATCH A *MOVIE!*
DEAL!
DEAL!
DEAL!
THE END

WATCH OUT FOR PAPERCUT™

Welcome to the frightful final pages of HOTEL TRANSYLVANIA #2 "My Little Monster-Sitter," the gruesome giggle-inducing graphic novel by "Spooky" Stefan Petrucha, writer, and Allen "Ghostly" Gladfelter and Zazo "the Zombie," artists, from "Petrifying" Papercutz—those batty boys and ghouls dedicated to publishing great graphic novels for all ages. I'm Jim "Screaming" Salicrup, Editor-in-Chief and Substitute Bellhop at the HOTEL TRANSYLVANIA. I'm here to once again share a personal behind-the-scenes story and recommend a few Papercutz graphic novels. First, the behind-the-scenes story…

As a kid growing up a long, long time ago, I was always looking for ways to earn a little extra money. You see, I was addicted to comicbooks, and every week I had to get another fix. (I still do! Just ask Ted and Ingrid at my favorite comicbook store.) And for that I needed moolabux, dough, *mucho dinero*—in other words, cold hard cash. After all, a comicbook was about 12 cents an issue back then, 25 cents for the double-size annuals (I told you it was a long, long time ago). I did whatever I could to supplement my 25-cents-a-week allowance. I carried grocery bags for tips. I shined shoes. I searched for deposit bottles to cash in. But my favorite gig was babysitting. One of my neighbors would hire me to baby sit their infant son, and I'd have their whole apartment to myself—and the best part was, the father was a comics fan who worked downtown, and he'd get the new comics a full week ahead of when they would arrive in the neighborhood. The kid was a real dream to take care of compared to Wanda and Wayne's wolf pups, but well, with great power must also come great responsibility, and I'm proud to say, there was never any mishaps, and everything turned out well.

Speaking of old comicbooks, Papercutz has probably published the most unexpected comics revival of the year—MANOSAURS! Two virtually forgotten comicbooks, MANOSAURS #0 (Yeah, that was a thing!) and #1, were published back in the 1900s—1993 to be precise. The MANOSAURS were created by Stuart Fischer, and was about these out-of-time characters that were published way ahead of their time. Now the MANOSAURS are back, courtesy of "Spooky" Stefan Petrucha, writer, and Yellowhale, artists. MANOSAURS is the story of Denise and Leo "Doc" Jeffries, down on their luck proprietors of the dumpy Dynamic Dino Display museum, and what happens when "Doc" unearths a box of bona fide dinosaur eggs in their backyard. These eggs hatch four talking dinosaurs that rapidly adapt and grow into their new environment, becoming Tri, Rex, Ptor, and Pterry, human/dinosaur hybrids called MANOSAURS, with the personalities of typical teenagers. MANOSAURS is available now at your favorite booksellers. Check out the preview on the following pages.

Back to HOTEL TRANSYLVANIA, we're sure you noticed that this time around we're offering up an all-new story based on HOTEL TRANSYLVANIA THE SERIES. In HOTEL TRANSYLVANIA #3, we'll be back to presenting a new story inspired by the movie series. It's called "Motel Transylvania," and wait till you see why! We hope you enjoyed your stay at HOTEL TRANSYLVANIA and hope you return soon.

Thanks,

Jim

MANOSAURS © 2018 Stuart Fischer and Paercutz.

STAY IN TOUCH!

EMAIL: salicrup@papercutz.com
WEB: papercutz.com
INSTAGRAM: @papercutzgn
TWITTER: @papercutzgn
FACEBOOK: PAPERCUTZGRAPHICNOVELS
FAN MAIL: Papercutz, 160 Broadway, Suite 700, East Wing, New York, NY 10038

Special Preview of MANOSAURS #1 "Walk Like a Manosaur

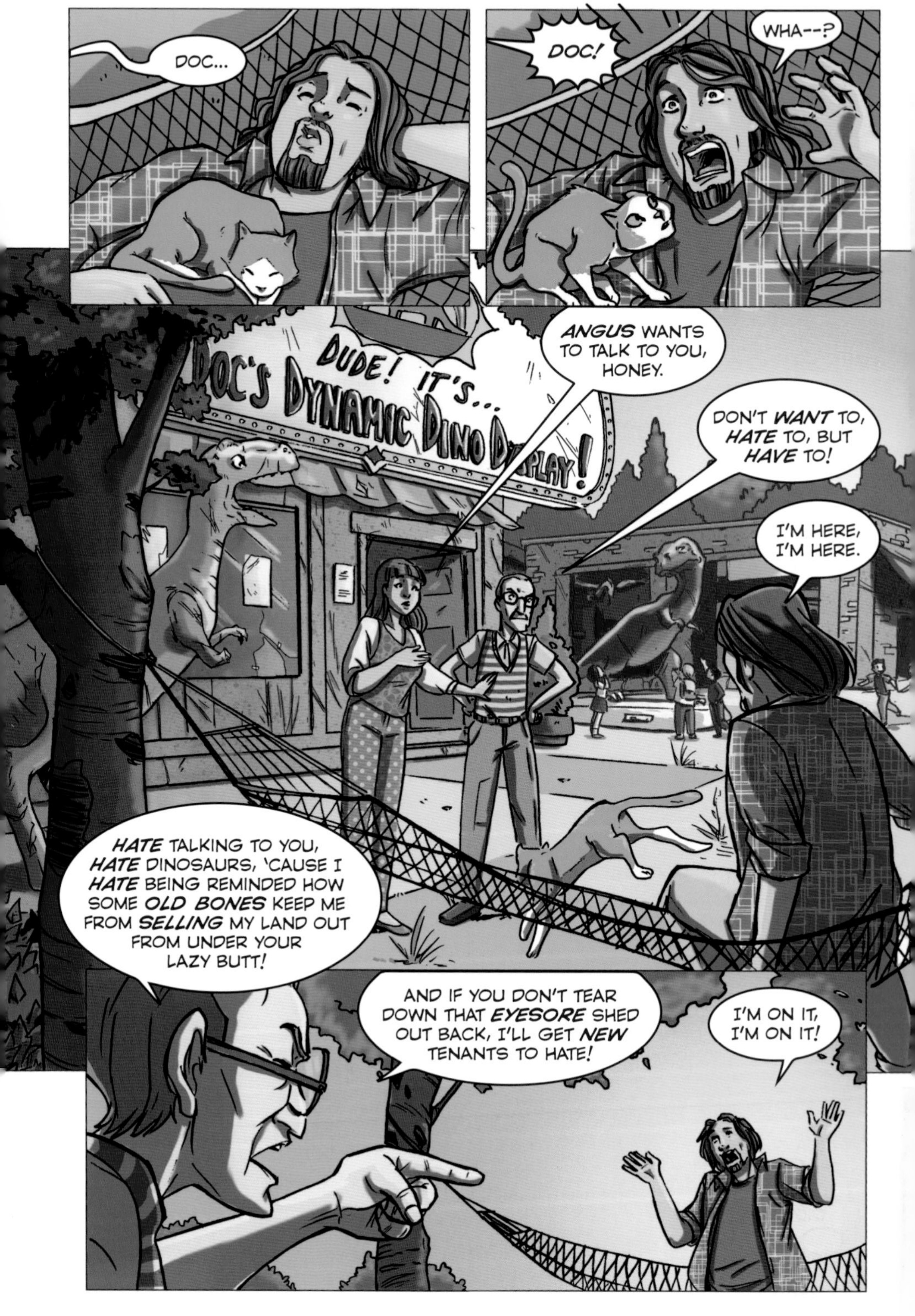
DOC...
DOC!
WHA--?
DUDE! IT'S... DOC'S DYNAMIC DINO DISPLAY!
ANGUS WANTS TO TALK TO YOU, HONEY.
DON'T WANT TO, HATE TO, BUT HAVE TO!
I'M HERE, I'M HERE.
HATE TALKING TO YOU, HATE DINOSAURS, 'CAUSE I HATE BEING REMINDED HOW SOME OLD BONES KEEP ME FROM SELLING MY LAND OUT FROM UNDER YOUR LAZY BUTT!
AND IF YOU DON'T TEAR DOWN THAT EYESORE SHED OUT BACK, I'LL GET NEW TENANTS TO HATE!
I'M ON IT, I'M ON IT!

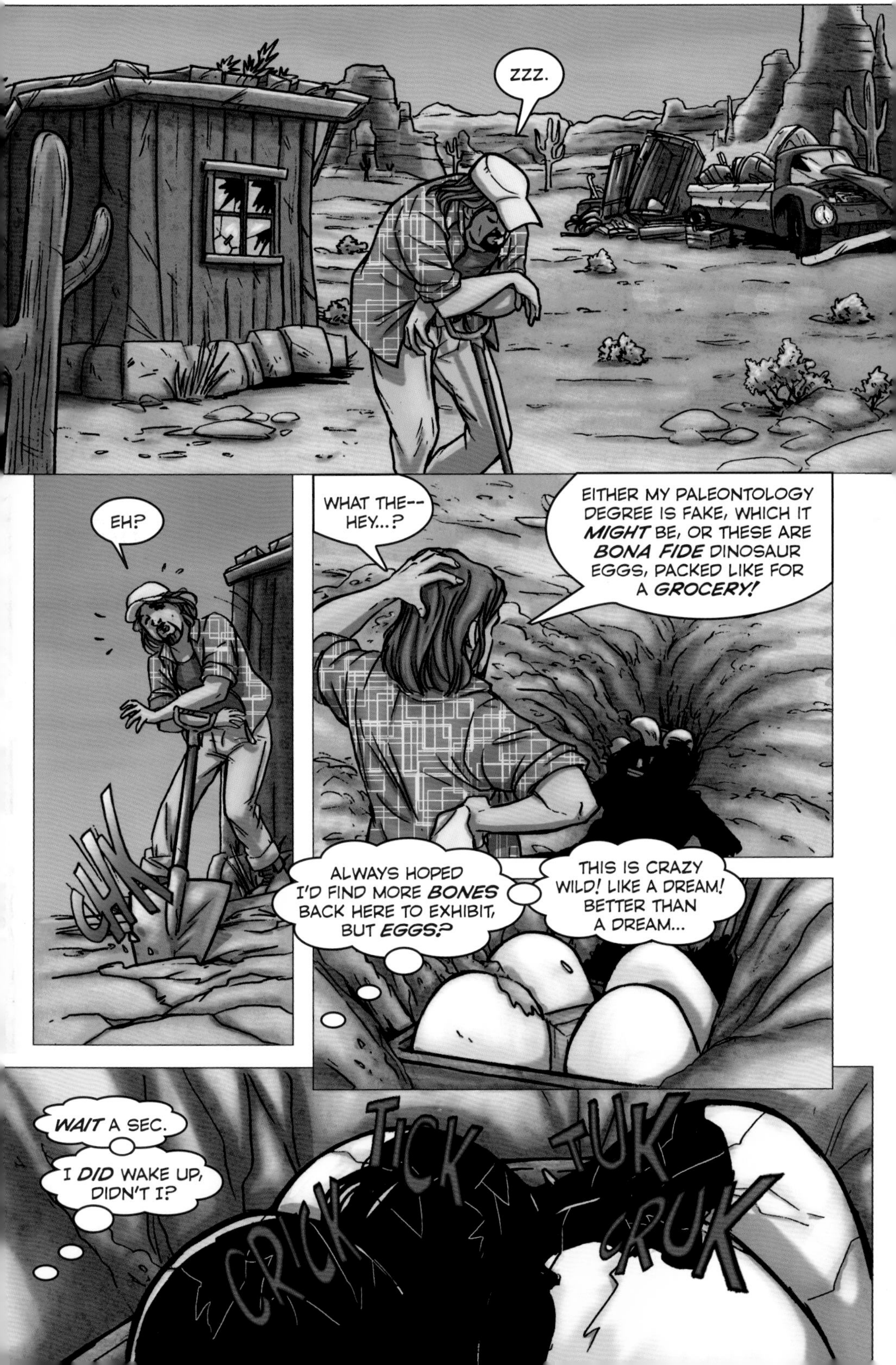
ZZZ.
EH?
CHUK
WHAT THE-- HEY...?
EITHER MY PALEONTOLOGY DEGREE IS FAKE, WHICH IT *MIGHT* BE, OR THESE ARE *BONA FIDE* DINOSAUR EGGS, PACKED LIKE FOR A *GROCERY!*
ALWAYS HOPED I'D FIND MORE *BONES* BACK HERE TO EXHIBIT, BUT *EGGS?*
THIS IS CRAZY WILD! LIKE A DREAM! BETTER THAN A DREAM...
WAIT A SEC.
I *DID* WAKE UP, DIDN'T I?
CRICK
TICK
TUK
CRUK

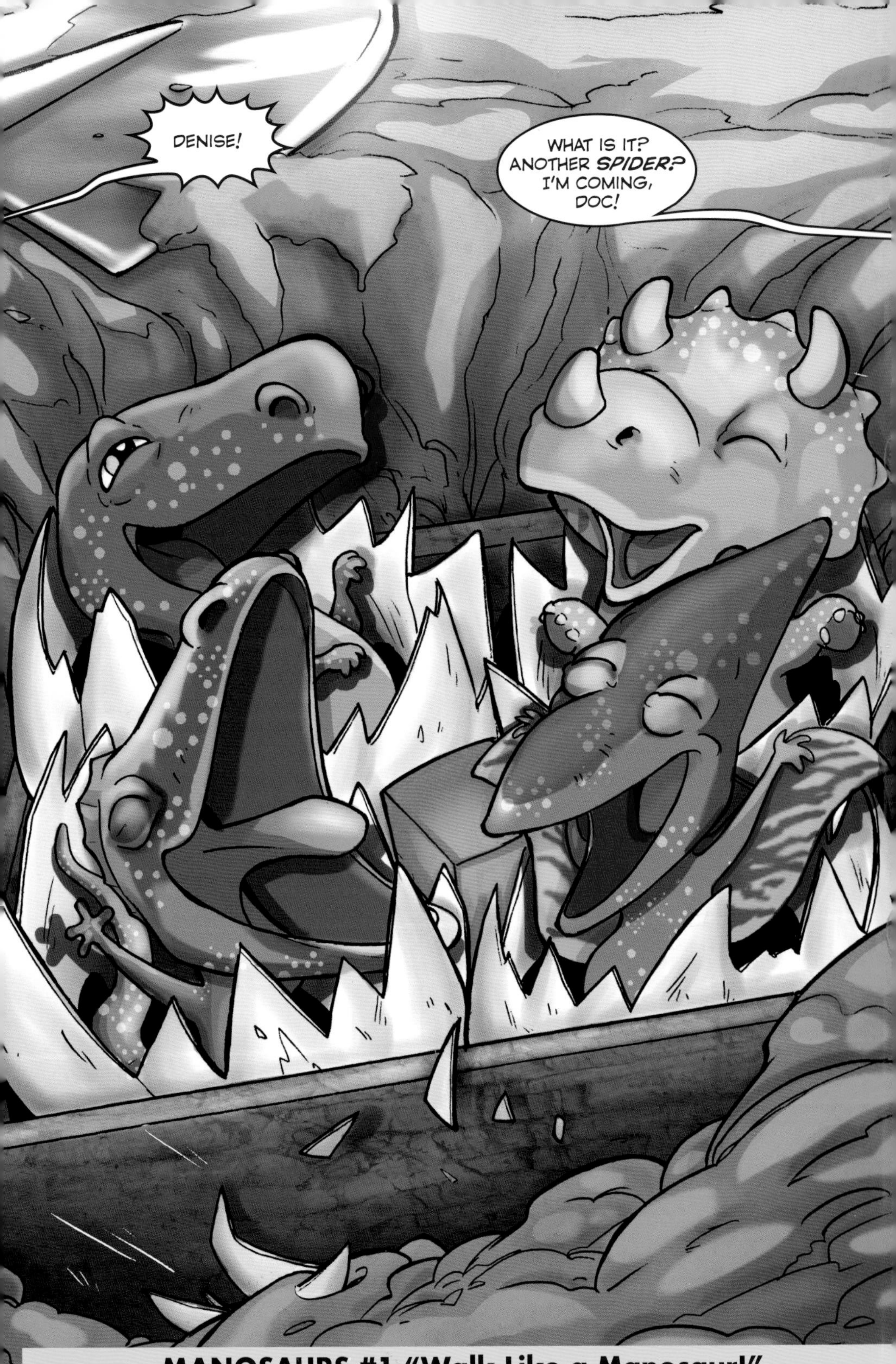
DENISE!
WHAT IS IT? ANOTHER SPIDER? I'M COMING, DOC!